D1642788

Blue Skies

Also from Dee Davis

Blue Skies
By Dee Davis

Rising Storm
Season 2
Episode 8

Story created by Julie Kenner and Dee Davis

EVIL EYE
CONCEPTS

Blue Skies, Episode 8
Rising Storm, Season 2
Copyright 2016 Julie Kenner and Dee Davis Oberwetter
ISBN: 978-1-945920-04-2

Published by Evil Eye Concepts, Incorporated

All rights reserved. No part of this book may be reproduced, scanned, or distributed in any printed or electronic form without permission. Please do not participate in or encourage piracy of copyrighted materials in violation of the author's rights.

This is a work of fiction. Names, places, characters, and incidents are the product of the author's imagination and are fictitious. Any resemblance to actual persons, living or dead, events or establishments is solely coincidental.

Acknowledgments from the Author

I've always believed in dreaming big. But I've learned over my lifetime that dreaming big isn't the same as making it so. And when Julie and I first started discussing the idea of creating Storm, Texas, while I fell in love with our creation, I wasn't certain we'd be able to bring it fully to fruition. I was wrong. Taking the reins from our initial imaginings for the series, the wonderful writers who make up the first season episodes have breathed amazing life into every character. And these imaginary people who have become so close to my heart have become real, not just to me but to readers as well.

For that I have to thank the amazing Julie Kenner, the best friend and business partner a girl could ever have! Without her, none of this would exist! And both Liz Berry and MJ Rose for their belief in this project and the tireless hours they have spent making sure everything is just right. And of course the first and second season authors: Lexi Blake, Elisabeth Naughton, Jennifer Probst, Larissa Ione, Rebecca Zanetti, RK Lilley, and Lisa Mondelo.

Foreword

Dear reader –

We have wanted to do a project together for over a decade, but nothing really jelled until we started to toy with a kernel of an idea that sprouted way back in 2012 ... and ultimately grew into Rising Storm.

We are both excited about and proud of this project—not only of the story itself, but also the incredible authors who have helped bring the world and characters we created to life.

We hope you enjoy visiting Storm, Texas. Settle in and stay a while!

Happy reading!

Julie Kenner & Dee Davis

Sign up for the Rising Storm/1001 Dark Nights Newsletter and be entered to win an exclusive lightning bolt necklace specially designed for Rising Storm by Janet Cadsawan of Cadsawan.com.

Go to www.RisingStormBooks.com to subscribe.

As a bonus, all subscribers will receive a free
Rising Storm story
Storm Season: Ginny & Jacob – the Prequel
by Dee Davis

Chapter 1

Celeste Salt sucked in a fortifying breath and looked at herself in the mirror. Her hair was passable, her make-up concealing the worst of the dark circles beneath her eyes. Unfortunately, there was nothing to be done for the gauntness in her cheeks or the deep lines now etched around her mouth and eyes.

Grief was an insidious thing. Digging in and holding you down, even when you knew in your heart that you needed to push forward. Celeste had always been a fighter. It was something her children had admired. And then somewhere along the way she'd lost her path, Jacob's death seemingly sealing her fate.

But no more. There was still life ahead of her. Maybe it wouldn't be the stellar ride into the sunset she and Travis had planned all those years ago. But that didn't mean there wasn't something left to be salvaged. To be lived.

Her daughter Lacey was right. It was time to move on. Step by cautious step. She forced a smile, the face in the mirror shifting with the motion, looking almost pretty. Almost. Squaring her shoulders, Celeste walked from the bathroom into the bedroom. And after pulling a manila envelope from deep inside her lingerie drawer, she made her way downstairs.

It was early, most of the house's residents still sleeping. It was comforting somehow to know that her daughter was safe and sound in her room. And that her sister and her children also slept nearby. Payton had always been her rock. And now it was time to return the favor. But first up she needed to clean house. If she was going to survive, she had to get rid of the garbage. No matter how much it hurt.

"I wasn't expecting you up this morning." Her husband looked up from the kitchen table where he was reading the paper. Some things at least were predictable. Travis never went anywhere without a cup of coffee. Once, long ago, in what now seemed like another life, she'd been up with the sun, making sure his coffee was hot and waiting when he'd come downstairs fresh from a shower.

But those days were gone.

And finally...finally she understood that nothing was going to bring them back.

"I wanted to talk to you." She poured herself a cup of coffee and sat across from him at the table, laying the manila envelope on the tabletop.

Travis frowned. "Is something wrong?" He paused, the frown deepening. "I mean, something more than usual."

"No. Nothing's changed." Except me, she wanted to scream. But instead she met his gaze, willing her courage to hold. This wasn't going to be easy. Travis was part of her. He'd given her a life. A home. Children. But then maybe she had it wrong. Maybe she'd given *him* those things. Maybe he'd been lucky to have her.

Or maybe they'd been lucky to have each other. At least in the beginning.

"Then what?" he asked, sounding impatient. He always sounded impatient these days. Sadly, Celeste knew why. And it had nothing to do with their son's death; his impatience with her, with their life, it had started long before that. And if Jacob had lived, they'd already have had this conversation.

But her son was dead and Celeste had lost herself in grief. Only now it was time to push the pain aside and face things head on. Jacob would want that. Lacey did want that. And Payton had done just that. There were no two ways about it—it was long past time for Celeste to stand on her own two feet.

She swallowed, looking down at the envelope, drawing strength from what she knew it contained. "I know about Kristin, Travis."

He dropped the newspaper, the color leeching out of his face, his mouth working as he tried to find words. "Oh God, Celeste, I'm so sorry."

She shook her head, holding up her hand to cut him off. "Save it. I don't want to hear it. There's nothing you can say that is going to fix this. And you know that as well as I do." Her hands were shaking, and she pulled them down to her lap, interlacing her fingers to try and hold onto her control.

"Darling, you're not well. We don't need to do this now."

She pulled in a deep breath, forcing herself to meet his gaze. "Yes, Travis. We do."

He shifted in his chair, clearly uncomfortable. Travis always liked things neat and tidy. Everything in its proper place. It's why she'd spent practically her entire marriage making sure that everything was always perfect, reasoning that if he was happy, she was happy.

What a load of crap.

"How did you find out?" he asked, still frowning.

"It doesn't matter. It just matters that I know."

"How long then? How long have you known? Is that why you've been so...so..." He trailed off, clearly unwilling to finish the sentence.

"Crazy? Drunk? Lost?" She bit out the words. "No. That was because of Jacob. Because he was important to my life. I've known about Kristin since before he died. And had the car accident never happened, then maybe this whole thing would have played out differently. Maybe we would have found a way to work things thorough, but Jacob is gone and anything left I had to give, he took with him. So here we are, sitting in our kitchen, pretending like there's still something to talk about."

"But, Celeste," he protested, "no matter what I've done, you have to know that I love you."

"No, you don't." She shook her head, feeling the tears prick the back of her eyes. "Maybe you did once upon a time, but not anymore. Not for a long time. And while I can't pretend that it doesn't hurt, I can at least return the favor." She stared at him, some tiny part of her wishing that there were a way to stop this. To turn back the clock. To fix whatever it was they'd broken so long ago. But deep in her heart she knew it wasn't possible. That moment, if it had ever existed, was long past. "Travis, I don't love you anymore either."

Silence stretched through the kitchen, memories playing like a movie inside Celeste's head. She and Travis laughing as they'd sat down for their first breakfast in the new house. Holding hands across the table while baby Sara Jane cried and cried. Jacob running into the room, flushed with pride over a Little League victory. Lacey, covered in flour, proud of the very first, albeit lopsided, cake she'd ever baked. This had been a family kitchen. Still was a family kitchen.

But whatever connection had existed between the two of them—it was now severed beyond hope.

"You don't mean that." He actually looked hurt. The thought surprised Celeste.

"I do. You've always thought you could have everything your way. Keep your life compartmentalized so that you could have it all. But it doesn't work like that, Travis. Life is messy and things happen. And people change. I don't know why we let it go. But we did, and there's no going back. And even if there were, I don't want to." She pushed the envelope across the table. "I had these drawn up a couple weeks before Jacob died."

Travis took the envelope and opened the clasp holding it closed. He slid out the papers and scanned the contents. "You're divorcing me?" Again she was amazed at his shock.

"Surely you're not surprised? I mean, to be honest, if Jacob had lived, it's entirely possible that you'd have beaten me to the draw. Or were you planning to live your double life forever?" The idea was repugnant, but she suddenly realized that this was exactly what Travis had been planning to do. She could see it in his eyes.

"What about the girls?" he asked. "Are you sure you want to do this to them?"

"They're strong. They'll be fine."

"But with everything that's happened. Jacob…"

"Don't you dare throw our son's death at me like that. We've all been through hell. But like Lacey said, it's time to come out the other side. And I can't do that if you're still here—living in this house, carrying on with her."

"It's not like that, Celeste. I mean I truly care about her."

"Good. Then you'll have someone in your life. I don't want you to be miserable, Travis. I just don't want you here anymore. I need to focus on the people who love me. On Sara Jane and Lacey."

"This is because of Payton, isn't it? She left Sebastian so now you're leaving me."

"No. This is about your infidelity and the fact that we don't love each other. I'm not even angry at you anymore. I'm just tired. And I'm drowning in grief. And the only way I can survive is if I clean up my life. And to do that, I need you gone. I need you to sign these papers and walk out the door. Go to Kristin. Go with my blessing. Just go."

She picked up a pen and handed it to him.

"Sign it, Travis. Set us free."

For a moment his eyes softened, and she saw a hint of the man she'd fallen in love with all those years ago, and then his jaw tightened and he flipped the papers to the signature page, signing his name with a flourish.

"There," he said, pushing the papers back to her. "It's done."

She nodded, not certain she trusted herself to speak.

"I'll send for my things." He stood up and took his jacket from the back of the chair and slipped it on. "Do you want to tell the girls together?"

She shook her head. "No. I'd prefer to do it separately. I promise I won't malign you. I won't lie, but I don't want your relationship with your daughters to suffer because of our failings."

He nodded, grabbed his keys from the bowl beside the refrigerator, and then pulled open the back door.

This is it, she thought, her fingers tightening together. The end of her marriage.

"Celeste," Travis said, turning to face her one last time. "I never meant to hurt you. I truly did love you, you know."

"Maybe so," she sighed, her eyes surprisingly dry. "But it wasn't enough."

* * * *

Marisol Moreno pulled a pan of muffins from the oven, her mind turning over the events of last night's dinner with Patrick Murphy. They'd finally been truly honest with each other. After over a year of dancing around the idea of becoming closer, they'd finally accepted the fact that it just wasn't meant to be. She'd been so afraid she'd hurt him. That he'd not understand her inability to commit one way or the other. But as usual he'd been insightful and thoughtful and well...totally Patrick.

If only she had been able to fall in love with him. It would be a heck of a lot easier than having fallen for a man who wasn't even going to stay in town. But still, just the thought of Ian Briggs sent heat coursing through her. The man made her want things she hadn't thought about since before her parents died. And that had been a long, long time.

It wasn't as if they'd done anything about it. A lot of flirting, but no dates and no talk of anything that might suggest there was a relationship in the offing. And Marisol understood why. Ian's life was in Montana. He clearly cared about Marcus, but that didn't mean he was going to pull up stakes and move here. And Marisol's life was completely and irrevocably in Storm. She had Luis and Ginny, and, soon enough, the baby to take care of.

Her family just kept growing and they needed her. That much of her protestation to Patrick Murphy had been true. She didn't have time for a relationship. So maybe it was just as well that Ian was only passing through.

Still, a wicked part of her mind whispered, *while he was here...*

She shook her head, grabbed a tray full of cookies, and walked out of the kitchen and into the main part of her bakery,

Cuppa Joe. Best to quit thinking about what could never be and concentrate on what mattered. Her business and her family.

As if to contradict that pledge, Ian Briggs' deep laugh echoed through the room. He was sitting at a table in the corner with Marcus, their two dark heads bent together as Ian recounted some story or another. Just seeing him in her bakery had her shivering with need.

He looked up, his eyes meeting hers, and damned if he didn't wink. Almost as if he knew what she was thinking. Color stained her cheeks and she bent to place cookies inside the case, trying to ignore the fact that she was now flushed from head to toe. Damn the man. Clearly, she needed to get out more.

"Marisol," a soft voice called, interrupting her cascading thoughts. "When you get a chance, can we get another hit of coffee?"

Anna Mae Prager sat at the table closest to the counter, Chase Johnson next to her, their fingers intertwined. Talk about desire. It was thick enough to cut between the two of them. Never mind that they were both old enough to…Marisol cut off the thought. There wasn't such a thing as being too old. Hope was eternal and all that.

Marisol grabbed a pot and rounded the counter, swiftly filling their cups. Anna Mae was beaming. "You'll never guess what happened," she gushed, a smile breaking across her face.

Chase was grinning, too.

"Maybe not, but I'm hoping you'll tell me." At least it looked like it was good news. There'd been enough bad stuff happening in Storm lately to last a lifetime. It would be nice to have something to smile about.

Anna Mae stuck out her hand, a large pear-shaped diamond winking in the light. "Chase proposed. To me."

"Well, now, darlin', there's never been anyone else." The man of the moment grinned.

Anna Mae snorted. "Like I believe that."

Chase had the good sense to look embarrassed. "Okay, well, what I meant was that there's never been anyone else I've wanted to spend my life with." He frowned. "At least what there is left of it."

"Now, Chase, we agreed, we live for today. No worries about what tomorrow brings." Anna Mae's smile filled the room as she looked back to Marisol. "Can you believe it? We're getting married."

"I can't think of two more deserving people." Marisol grinned back at them, a tiny sliver of sadness piercing her heart. What if she never found this kind of joy?

"Did I hear you say you're getting hitched?" Ian asked, strolling over to the table as Marcus headed for the door.

"As soon as I can get her to the church," Chase said. "About time she made an honest man of me."

"I'd say this calls for a celebration. How about some of those cheese kolaches?" Ian tilted his head in the direction of the pastry case. "Marisol makes the best I've ever tasted."

"It's a lovely idea," Anna Mae said, coloring prettily as Chase grabbed her hand again. "But we've got to go. I need to tell my sister before the town crier announces it from the rooftops."

"In that case you'd better hurry," Marisol laughed. "Hedda Garten was in here when you told me, and she's already out the door and probably on the telephone spreading the news."

"Hedda never could hold on to a secret." Chase pushed back his chair and helped Anna Mae up. "We'll take a rain check on the kolaches."

"Absolutely," Marisol said. "And congratulations."

She watched as the two of them walked out of the shop, feeling Ian's heat beside her. He was big and tall, the kind of man who'd make a woman feel protected.

He'd led a hard life. Marcus had told her a little about his past. He'd lost a son. Murdered. And then he'd killed the man who'd done it. Not that Marisol blamed him. She'd have done the same if anyone had dared to hurt Luis or Ginny. In fact, she'd had many a fantasy about what she'd like to do to Senator Rush. Payback for being such a grade-A bastard.

Of course, she didn't actually have the cojones to see it through, but that didn't mean she didn't understand Ian's reasons.

"You still want that kolache?" she asked, trying not to sound too desperate. Truth was, she didn't want him to leave. Ever, if she were being truly honest.

"Don't mind if I do," he said. "Especially if you'll join me. Turns out I've got a little something to celebrate, too."

"Well, that's intriguing. Give me a second." She stepped behind the counter, grabbed a couple of kolaches and some more coffee. Then after a word with Delia Bruce, who was helping out until she found a full-time job, Marisol crossed back over to Ian's table, setting the plate and cups down as she slid into a seat. "So what's happened?"

Ian smiled, his eyes dark and full of something Marisol wasn't sure she wanted to put a name to. "I'm now the proud owner of a hundred and ten acres of prime grazing land about fifteen miles south of here."

"You're kidding. I knew you were looking for a place for Marcus, but to be honest, with the Johnsons' hold on everything to do with cattle around here, I figured it was a lost cause."

"Well, now, you see, I'm not the kind of man to give up without a fight." He paused, his gaze devouring her. "Especially when it's something I truly want."

Marisol swallowed too fast and almost choked on her coffee. Whoever decided cowboys had the power to make a girl swoon definitely had the right idea about things. At least when it came to Ian Briggs. "I see." She didn't. Not really. But she found herself wanting him to tell her.

"Zeke Johnson and I had a little talk and a meeting of the minds, you might say. And now Marcus and I have a chance to make a go of it here in Texas."

"Marcus and you..." She was sounding like a schoolgirl. Limited to repeating whatever he had to say. And to make matters worse, she'd managed to shred one of the kolaches.

"Marcus," he repeated, a slow, sexy smile tilting his lips. "And me. Me being the relevant part of this conversation. Me— and you, that is."

Marisol felt a shiver of something work its way down her

spine. "Me and you." Lord, she was still repeating.

"I'm hoping maybe we can have dinner tonight to celebrate?" he asked, his eyes full of laughter and something else. Something hotter. Something full of promise.

"Dinner would be great." Amazing. Fabulous. Wonderful. Her stomach actually clenched with excitement.

"It's a date then." He leaned over and before she even had time to think about it, brushed his lips against hers. She closed her eyes, relishing his touch.

"Marisol Moreno, I can't believe what I'm seeing."

Marisol sprang back, opening her eyes, coloring with guilt. Standing just across from her was her little brother Luis and his girlfriend Mallory, his eyes dancing with laughter.

"Kinda feels nice to have the shoe on the other foot." His grin turned mischievous.

"You show some respect for your sister, Luis," Ian admonished, not looking the slightest bit embarrassed for having been caught kissing in front of her brother.

"Oh, I have nothing but respect, Mr. Briggs. And if I'm honest, I'm totally psyched. It's about time Marisol let herself be happy. She's been way too busy trying to take care of me and my sister. Thinks she doesn't deserve her own life. But we know better, right?"

Marisol looked from a grinning Luis to Ian, who was clearly gloating. Mallory, who was standing behind Luis, waggled her eyebrows at Marisol and mouthed one word. "Men."

"It's Ian," Ian was saying to Luis as he motioned to the table's empty chairs. "Your sister was just helping me celebrate. Join us."

Marisol jumped up to get sodas for her brother and Mallory, her head swimming and her body still reacting to what had merely been a simple kiss. That and the fact that he'd asked her to dinner.

Of course, he was still leaving.

But now that he'd bought land in Texas, surely that meant he'd at least be visiting now and then. The relevant question being whether or not that was enough.

Truth be told, it wasn't.

But then maybe she'd be smart to just take what she could get. After all, a girl didn't have the chance to spend time with a man like Ian every day. A little bit was better than nothing. Right?

Her earlier joy evaporated as reality set in. Ian was the kind of man she could so easily lose her heart to. And anything he felt—well, it had to be temporary, didn't it? He knew she wasn't going to leave Storm. And she knew that eventually he'd be heading back to Montana.

Which left her where exactly?

Flirting with disaster.

Chapter 2

Sebastian Rush walked out of his office, wondering how the hell it had all come to this. He and Payton had an agreement, damn it. And it hadn't included walking out on him and taking his kids. His numbers had dipped five points in the polls. Thank God he'd already been reelected. Still, he didn't need this kind of pressure.

What he needed was some good news. Something that would cast him in a more positive light. His mother was always harping on spinning everything. Surely this could be spun as well. He shook his head, smiling at a group of passing ladies who averted their eyes as if he was a leper. When the hell had a man's sexual proclivities been questioned so stridently? JFK had had mistresses. Nobody gave a good goddamn. Hell, when Marilyn Monroe sang happy birthday to the man, it was positive press.

Of course, Marilyn hadn't been college aged. Or had she? Sebastian frowned and then immediately forced himself to relax his face muscles. The camera added years; no point in helping it along.

In just a few days he was heading back to Austin.

Alone.

Not that that wasn't normal. No, what wasn't normal was that there'd be no family waiting for him at home. No one to trot out in front of the journalists when family values were in play. Even as he had the thought, he knew it was too cold. Too calculating. He might have felt that way about his ice queen of a wife, but he loved his children.

Didn't he?

Jeffry was a disappointment certainly. Even in today's liberal atmosphere, surely Jeffry knew how his sexual orientation would play out in the media. Why in the world in the midst of all this scandal had he chosen now to come out of the damn closet?

Maybe it was just a fad. That's what his mother thought. Experimentation. The idea made Sebastian shudder. And if Jeffry's predilections weren't enough to deal with, there was Brittany's infatuation with Marcus Alvarez. A deviant offender of the first order. Not the kind of man he wanted to inherit his kingdom. And besides how could he condone a relationship between his daughter and the brother of the woman who'd practically destroyed his career singlehandedly?

At least the girl had fallen off the radar. A town pariah. No one was listening to her now. Although the damage was done. If he'd had his way, he would have destroyed her. But as usual his mother was right. The potential for fallout was too dangerous.

God what a clusterfuck.

What he needed was something to save the fucking day.

As if some twisted deity somewhere had heard his plea, Ginny Moreno walked out of the pharmacy, her belly so swollen she almost waddled. And yet, Sebastian felt himself grow hard.

He increased his pace, closing in behind her, relishing the chance to catch her off guard, a wild idea forming in his head. If his family had deserted him, maybe he'd just get a new one.

"Hold on there a minute, Ginny."

She stopped, startled, eyes wide as she turned around to face him. "What do you want?"

"To talk. We haven't had a chance to talk lately." He smiled, pouring on the charm. It's what he excelled at after all. "I've been doing a lot of thinking."

"I'll bet you have," Ginny said, the words half mumbled.

"About us, I mean." He reached out to touch her elbow, and she jerked free, eyes flashing. He didn't remember her being so self-assured. It excited him. With a little polish... He shook his head, forcing himself to concentrate. "I'm sorry. I didn't mean to invade your space; I just was hoping maybe we could try to start over."

"Start over?" She actually looked puzzled. "And do what? Look, I don't know what you're angling for here. But I told you before, I don't need your help and I've no interest in you being a part of this child's life."

"I see you've grown tougher than you were when we were together."

"It isn't like I had a choice." She took a step backward, but he quickly closed the distance.

"No, I suppose you didn't. I admire that about you though. Most women would have caved in your situation. But not you. You've stood strong. I know that the Murphy kid abandoned you. Hell, I did too, at first. But now—"

"There is no now," Ginny said, her chin lifting up in defiance as he moved even closer, the back of a building keeping her from stepping farther back. "I want nothing to do with you. You're just a perverted old man who gets off using young women."

He lifted his hand, wanting to slap her words away, but forced himself to close his fingers instead. If he hit her, it was all over. "Ginny, I understand why you're angry. I was wrong. I shouldn't have abandoned you when the truth came out. But I'm trying to make amends for it now."

"By taking my baby?" She was clenching her fists, her breath coming in short pants. God, despite the fact that she was pregnant as hell, he still wanted her.

"No. I shouldn't have threatened you before." In truth, he had no regrets, except that Payton had betrayed him and now he was forced to regroup. He forced a soothing smile. "I meant by taking care of both of you."

For a moment she just stared up at him, her soft breath fanning his face, and he started to smile in triumph. This was why he won elections. All he had to do was say the right words, give the right smile, and anything—anything was his.

He reached out to touch her, but she jerked sideways, breaking free of him. Her eyes flashed as she narrowed them in determination. "Not a chance in hell, Senator Rush."

Anger sparked as he saw his chance for victory slipping away. The little bitch, how dare she reject him? He grabbed her arm, swinging her back to face him, not caring that they were standing on a public street. "You're not walking away from me that easily, Ginny. You're carrying my baby. Mine. And I don't think it would take all that much for me to convince a judge to give me custody. I mean, what have you got to offer a child?" She might be the mother, but he was a senator. Hell, he was Sebastian Rush and that meant a hell of a lot more than any claim some little nobody like her might have on the kid.

He shook her, his anger making him reckless. "I have everything. A name. Money. Power. And you—you have nothing. You're a no-name little whore from the wrong side of the tracks in a backwater town. You'll never be a match for me. So you think about that. And then you think about whether you'd rather have me as a friend." He tightened his hand on her arm as he ran a finger over the curve of one breast. "Or an enemy. It's your choice, Ginny. So you think about it."

He held her gaze for a moment longer, satisfied to see a flicker of fear in her eyes, then let her go and turned and walked away.

Stupid cunt. If she didn't want to play nice, then she'd find out what happened when he played dirty.

* * * *

"It's a little early for that, isn't it, son?" Sonya Murphy walked into the bar from the back room, a tray of clean glasses in her hands. Dillon followed on her heels, a keg on his shoulder.

Logan looked over the top of his beer at his mother and brother. Just what he needed, family interference. Of course, that was part and parcel for the Murphy clan. He knew because he'd gone halfway around the world to escape them, only to realize how damn much he missed their constant meddling once he was gone.

"I'm just trying to sort out a few things." Truth be told, he'd been trying to sort things out ever since he'd left Delia Bruce and her sage advice at her front gate. Hell, he'd have been better off if he'd never gone out with her at all. Damn Marcus and Brittany. Interfering friends were worse than family—almost.

"Listen, bro, I don't think you're going to find answers in the bottom of a glass."

"Says the publican's son." Logan scowled at his brother who only laughed as he shoved the keg under the counter.

"Pot calling kettle black," Dillon returned. But at least his brother had the decency to fill a glass and sit down beside him. Logan's mother, on the other hand, didn't look too pleased with either of her sons.

Still, she poured herself a cup of coffee and came to stand in front of them, still behind the bar. "The two of you are so much like your father."

"I don't see that as a problem," Logan said, as Dillon grunted in agreement.

"Most of the time, neither do I." Sonya's smile was warm. "He does, after all, hold the key to my heart. But that doesn't mean the man's a saint."

"Thank the good Lord," Dillon said, raising his glass. "He already thinks he's right all the time; can you imagine how hard it would be to live with him if he were truly perfect?"

"Don't speak ill of your father." She shot her oldest son a quelling glance. "The point I'm making is that your father almost let me slip out of his grasp. If he hadn't fought for me, I'd have married Marshall Beckham."

It was an old story, one that differed slightly depending on if his mother or father was telling the tale. But the facts were that Marshall Beckham had wanted Sonya for his own. And a more determined man there'd never been. Except for Aiden Murphy.

"We know the story, Ma." Dillon rolled his eyes, shooting a look at Logan.

"So you do. But you're missing the obvious point. If your father had let himself be swayed by all the gossip—lies started by

Marshall himself—none of us would be standing here right now. He had to reach past all the bullhockey and take what he wanted." She shrugged and took a sip of coffee, her gaze holding theirs. "Me."

"And you're trying to tell Logan that he should wade through the shit and get Ginny back?"

"Except that it's real shit," Logan protested. "Not fabricated lies. Or at least the lies were what created the shit in the first place. And to make it worse, they were Ginny's." Logan tried for anger, but his heart wasn't in it. Delia had been right. He did love Ginny. And the idea of living a life without her made his gut hurt.

"Okay, so maybe my analogy isn't quite right," his mother said. "But the point is, life is short and you have to go and get what you want. And sometimes to do that, you have to sacrifice your pride."

"That's pretty much what Delia said to me." Logan sighed.

"Well, that complicates things a bit, don't you think," Dillon said, his words a statement, not a question.

"More than you know, brother. But not in the way you mean. Ginny saw us together."

"You and Delia?" his mother asked. "That can't have gone well."

"I don't know. Brittany talked to her, but I felt like a total ass. To both of them, if that matters. I just don't know what to do."

"About Delia or Ginny?" Dillon quipped, but sobered when Logan shot him an angry look.

"Ginny."

"Do you love her?" his mother asked, her voice gentle as she reached over to cover his hand with hers.

"I do. It's just that I thought she was the one person who would never lie to me."

"I don't condone what she did, telling people the baby was Jacob's. But I can understand why she did it. And I think if you're honest with yourself, so can you. Sometimes all it takes is a beginning. A first step." Sonya topped off her coffee and headed back toward the kitchen.

"See, I told you she was talking about you," Dillon offered as he took a sip of beer.

"Don't get too high on your horse, Dillon Murphy." Sonya stopped and turned around to face her sons again. "You've got to find your own kind of courage. If you truly love Joanne Alvarez, you can't let her stay in that hellhole Hector's made for her. She may feel trapped again now that he's home, but it's up to you to remind her that there's a way out. Or barring that, you can always run the bastard out of town again."

She walked past the bar and into the kitchen, leaving her two sons sitting for a moment in brooding silence.

Finally Logan turned to Dillon, a smile twitching at the corners of his mouth. "She always does know everything, our ma."

* * * *

Ginny leaned against the stone façade of the store next to Cuppa Joe, trying not to throw up. Her sister's bakery was only a few steps away. All she had to do was get there. But her head was swimming, the senator's words echoing in her head like some nightmarish litany. She'd made such a horrible mistake and now she was going to pay for it the rest of her life.

Not because she was having a child. That part she'd come to see as a blessing. No, it was the senator that made it all so hellish. He stopped at nothing to get what he wanted. And if he wanted Ginny's child, well he just might have the power and connections to pull it off.

She summoned a deep breath, ignoring the tightness in her chest and the pain in her lower back. This was not the place to have a panic attack. Just a few more steps. But even as her feet started to obey, her gut clenched in agony.

"Ginny." Her brother's voice reached her from what seemed to be a great distance, but she felt his hand on her elbow. "Hang on there, sis. We're almost to Marisol's." He tightened his hold as Mallory came up, supporting her from the other side.

Everything seemed to run together after that. Mallory and Luis propelled her forward, her little brother holding her tightly, giving her his strength. Then the cool air of Cuppa Joe hit her face and she instantly felt better, the familiar sounds and smells of Marisol's bakery easing her pain. Her gut relaxed, and the senator's voice was banished to some dark corner of her brain.

Ian Briggs was there, lifting her with ease into his arms and carrying her over to the corner, away from the regulars sipping their late-morning coffee. Marisol hovered for a moment, her hand cool against Ginny's forehead. Then she disappeared, Ian's worried face swimming into view. It was nice to see him here. She'd seen the way he looked at Marisol. Like the sun rose and set around her. She tried to smile, but the effort cost too much. Logan had looked at her like that once upon a time.

"Maybe it's sunstroke," Ian was saying. "It's awfully hot for this time of year."

"Welcome to Texas, Ian." Ginny heard Marisol laugh as she handed her a glass of iced herbal tea. "Here you go, sweetie. Drink this. It'll help calm you down. And then you can tell us what's wrong."

"Is it Logan?" Luis asked, his face scrunched up in anger. "If it is, I'll break a few bones."

Laughter bubbled up in Ginny's throat but didn't actually make any sound. Still, it was funny to think of Luis trying to beat up Logan. Not that her brother was a wimp or anything, but Logan was a badass. A *trained* badass.

She swallowed the passionfruit tea, the cool liquid soothing. "Not Logan." Well, not completely anyway.

"Then what?" Marisol asked, pushing a plate of snickerdoodles in front of her. Marisol believed any problem could be made better if she threw enough cookies at it.

Ginny closed her eyes for a second, the senator's threats coming back full center. She hated to burden her family, but then what else was family for? She knew they'd stand by her. And peripherally Mallory was family too, and hadn't she just been hoping the same about Ian? Her gut clenched again, her back still aching.

She blew out a breath and opened her eyes. "It was Senator Rush." It seemed weird to be so formal. The guy had, in all probability, knocked her up. But Ginny realized she'd never really thought of him in any other way. How sick was that?

"What about him?" Marisol asked, her voice tight with anger. Ian reached over to lay a soothing hand on her shoulder. Yup. The man had it bad.

"He threatened me." Ginny's voice came out on a whisper, and she shuddered with the memory. "I think he was trying to get me to reconcile with him. Give him access to the baby."

"And you told him no," Luis said, crossing his arms over his chest, his expression thunderous.

"Of course I did. But that's when he threatened me." After another sip of tea and a wince from the pain in her gut, she told them everything the senator had said.

"I'll talk to him," Ian said, anger glittering from his eyes.

"No." Marisol shook her head. "This isn't your battle."

"The hell it isn't." Again he reached out to touch her, and for a brief moment Marisol leaned into the touch.

"No one is going to do anything." The pain had let up a bit, the tea and the proximity of her family easing her panic. "We don't even know if the baby is his."

"Ginny," Marisol began, but Ginny cut her off.

"I know the odds, Marisol. But I'm not giving up. And even if Little Bit turns out to be the senator's, I'm not just going to hand him or her over. This is my child. And he or she belongs here with me." Her gaze moved to encompass them all. "With us."

"And we'll do everything in our power to make sure that happens," Marisol said.

"Damn right," Ian echoed, with Luis and Mallory nodding behind him.

Ginny felt the warmth of her family surround her and started to relax, but then the pain was back, stronger now, almost robbing her of breath. She leaned forward, clutching her belly.

"So what do we do now?" Luis was asking.

Marisol's arms came around Ginny, holding her close. "We get Ginny to the hospital. I could be wrong, but I think that was a contraction."

Chapter 3

Joanne Alvarez shot a look over her shoulder at the closed master bedroom door. No sign of activity. Hector was still asleep. He'd been up long enough to demand his breakfast, but then headed back to bed the minute the last of the eggs had slid down his throat.

She'd finished the dishes and cleaned up the kitchen. Everything looked spotless. Although she knew that wasn't necessarily enough to placate her husband. Especially when he was angry and hung over, which was most of the time. Thankfully, Dakota was still sleeping, Mallory had left early, and Marcus was spending as little time at home as possible.

She hated the idea that her son was angry with her, that he believed she succumbed to Hector's rages out of fear. There was some truth to that, of course, but it was more than that. What she wanted more than anything in this lifetime was to protect her children. All three of them.

Dakota might not incite Hector's wrath as much as she and Marcus did, but he was doing his best to destroy her just the same. In some ways, she was the child most in danger. As long as Joanne kept Mallory safe and Marcus out of jail, the two of them would be fine. They'd both grown into wonderful people who had opportunities for real happiness. But Dakota. She wore her anger much like her father. And although Joanne knew there was a lonely, hurting girl inside, that part of her daughter was growing smaller and weaker every day.

And as long as Hector ran roughshod over the family, there

was every chance it would die out altogether. Joanne's eyes welled with tears and she wondered how the hell she'd come to this point? Why one mistake had turned into such a complete and total nightmare. Hector had been so charming. So handsome. He'd swept Joanne off her feet.

Oh, if she were honest, there had been signs. But she'd been young and stupid and Hector had been different. Exciting. Deadly. In the beginning, she'd thought she could change him. That loving him would make him whole. But there'd never been a chance for that. Hector wasn't interested in changing. And he sure as heck didn't love her.

But by the time she'd figured that out, it was too late. She was married with a toddler and another baby on the way. Her lot in life set in stone. He'd isolated her from her friends and family. He'd stolen her confidence. Her joy. And her life had become an endless game of save the children.

But then he'd gone away, and her life had been so much better. She'd pulled herself together. Had a glimpse of the woman she once was. The woman she was meant to be. But then, as if it were nothing but a cruel trick, Hector had jerked the rug out from under her again. She tried to tell herself that it was different. That her kids were older. Stronger. But she knew that if she tried to leave Hector, he'd take it out first on her and then on the people she loved.

Marcus, Mallory, even Dakota. And definitely on Dillon.

Dillon.

Despite the fact that Hector slept only a short distance away, her mind moved to thoughts of Dillon. She was still angry at him, but her heart wanted what it wanted. And she'd wanted Dillon Murphy for a very long time. She closed her eyes, allowing herself to think for a minute about his kisses.

Then she pushed the thoughts aside. There was no point in torturing herself over something she'd never have. Better to concentrate on her life as it was now. She straightened her skirt and checked her makeup in the hallway mirror. The cut on her lip was covered with lipstick and the bruise under her eye was almost concealed. The worst of her injuries were hidden by her clothes. And as long as she held her head high, there was a chance no one would notice.

It would be easier to stay here and lay low until she'd healed, until she'd defused at least a little of Hector's anger. But she wanted to talk to Tate. She needed to resign, but she wanted to do it in person. She knew he'd try to talk her out of it. But she simply couldn't risk Hector doing anything to upset the campaign. Tate deserved better than that.

All she had to do was nip down there before Hector woke up. Then on the way home, she'd stop by the grocery and tell him that's where she'd been. She picked up her purse and pulled out her keys, smiled weakly at her reflection, and then started for the front door.

"Where the hell do you think you're going?" Hector snarled, his hand closing around her upper arm, fingers digging into her skin.

She tried not to wince, but his grip was punishing.

"Out. We need milk," she whispered, trying to quell her roiling stomach.

"I'll get it. I don't want you going anywhere," he snarled. "Especially not dressed like that." His bloodshot eyes moved from her lips to her breasts. "You look like a whore. Dillon Murphy's whore." His grip tightened as he raised his fist, his face turning red as his anger crested.

Joanne closed her eyes, waiting for the blow.

* * * *

Payton Rush walked into the front hall of her sister's house, surprised to see Celeste sitting at the dining room table with a cup of coffee and a stack of stationery. Her sister looked tired, but she was dressed and sober, which was definitely an improvement. She finished writing something and then looked up with a wan smile.

"I would have come home sooner if I'd known you were going to be up and about." Payton crossed the hall and walked into the room, taking a seat across from her sister, trying to sound cheerful.

"I take it you stayed at Francine's last night?" The question was offhand, clearly nothing more than conversation.

"I did. And we had a lovely time," Payton returned, not sure that she should be saying the words out loud. Celeste was so fragile, but sitting here at the table, writing letters, her sister seemed almost normal. Whatever in the world that meant. "What are you doing?"

Celeste blew out a breath. "Writing thank you notes. So many people sent flowers and donations to honor Jacob. It's past time that I acknowledged the fact." She set her pen down. "In fact, it's past time I did a lot of things. I'm sorry for what I've put you through these last months. You had enough on your plate without having your baby sister fall to pieces too."

"Oh, Celeste, sweetie, I can't even imagine the pain you've been going through. If I'd lost Jeffry or Brittany, I'm not sure I could survive."

"You're a lot stronger than you give yourself credit for, Payton. Look what you did for Jeffry. And for Brittany. You showed them what a powerful woman can do. You stood up to Sebastian. And you circled around your children when they needed you."

"Yes, but you've always done that. I was too locked into my own little corner of hell to see the damage Sebastian and Marylee's skewed sense of morality was inflicting on my children. The truth is that you've been strong for years with a moment's weakness. And I've spent my life being weak and have had only a moment of strength."

Celeste reached over for Payton's hand. "The important thing is that we have each other. And our children." Her smile turned sly. "And Francine."

"Oh, stop it. I don't have her. I just am…well, we're feeling our way." Payton marveled at the fact that her sister had clued in to the newly minted relationship between her and Francine. Payton wasn't totally certain she understood it yet herself.

"*Feeling* being the operative word?" Celeste waggled her eyebrows, then sobered. "I'm happy for you. You deserve to have someone in your life who loves you for being you."

"So do you." Payton couldn't remember the last time she and Celeste had been so open and honest with each other. Tears touched her eyes. "So where do you go from here?"

"I don't really know. I'm going to take it minute by minute. Grief is a tricky thing. And I'm not going to pretend that I'm over it. I don't know that I'll ever get over losing Jacob. But I love my daughters and they need me now more than ever."

Payton paused, frowning as she realized what, or rather who, Celeste was omitting from their conversation. "What about Travis?"

Celeste lifted her chin. "We're getting divorced."

"Oh, Celeste, I'm so sorry." She wasn't surprised though. She'd known something was off with Travis. Been pretty sure he was having an affair, actually, though she hadn't wanted to know for sure.

"Don't be. It's long overdue. I actually had the papers drawn up before Jacob died."

She started to ask about the affair but then thought better of it. What if her sister didn't know? There was no need to add to her pain. "You did?"

"Yes." Celeste met her sister's gaze. "I knew about the affair, Payton."

Payton blew out a breath. "I wasn't sure if you'd heard."

Celeste's smile didn't reach her eyes. "I think half the town knows. It's next to impossible to keep a secret around here. Especially when Travis and Kristin are seen together all the time. They actually had the audacity to pass themselves off as a married couple at a resort in Bastrop."

"How in the world did you find out about that?"

"Friend of a friend saw them there. Kristin told her they were celebrating their anniversary. I thought Travis was at a convention in Austin. Color me stupid."

"Well, sadly, we're not the first women to have been cheated on by the men in our lives. And we won't be the last. But at least we're doing something about it. That's got to count for something. Right?"

"It counts for everything, Mom." Brittany walked into the dining room and laid her hand on Payton's shoulder.

"Brit, you scared me." Payton flashed a smile at her daughter. "I didn't hear you coming."

"Stealth, Mom. It's the name of the game." Brit laughed, then sobered, her attention turning to Celeste. "I'm so sorry, Aunt Celeste. But if it helps any, I think you're doing the right thing. Do Sara Jane and Lacey know?"

Celeste shook her head. "There hasn't been time. I only just told Travis this morning." She glanced down at her watch. "Heavens, it's almost noon. I need to fix us some lunch." She pushed to her feet then paused with a frown. "You won't say anything? Either of you? I mean, until I've had the chance to talk to the girls."

"Of course not." Payton was quick to reassure, Brittany nodding her agreement.

The front door slammed open as Mallory, Jeffry, and Lacey spilled in.

"The three of you look like you've been up to something," Payton observed with a smile.

"Well, not exactly," Lacey said, fidgeting as she looked to her mom. "But I do have something to tell you. Only I don't want to upset you."

"I'll be fine, honey. Whatever it is, we'll handle it together."

Lacey's gaze searched her mother's and then with a sigh she walked over to take her hands. "So Jeffry and I ran into Mallory on the driveway. She was coming to see us. To tell us something, I mean."

"Lacey," Celeste said, raising an eyebrow, the gesture so familiar that Payton wanted to cry. "Out with it."

"Okay." Lacey squeezed Celeste's hands and Payton held her breath. "The thing is, Mallory thought we should know." Lacey paused again, chewing on her lip as she watched her mother.

"Know what?" Celeste let out an exasperated sigh.

"About Ginny." Lacey's eyes lit with trepidation. "She's in labor."

* * * *

"I thought you were working today?" Logan said as his friend Marcus Alvarez strolled into the bar.

"I had a meeting with Ian, and then I had to pick up feed for Tucker, so I figured I might as well stop in here for some lunch."

"Sure. The usual?" Marcus was nothing if not predictable. At least when it came to food. At his friend's nod, he called the order through the window into the kitchen and then filled a glass with Shiner.

Marcus took the beer and had a long sip before wiping his mouth with his hand, a grin coasting across his face. "Much better. It's hotter than Hades out there. Doesn't feel like fall at all. Even for the Hill Country."

Logan poured himself a glass and settled at the bar with his friend. "So everything all right with Brittany?" He asked the question cautiously. He hadn't had the chance to talk to Marcus about the disastrous date with Delia Bruce. Or maybe he just hadn't wanted to discuss it. But the disappointment in Ginny's eyes would be branded on his heart forever. He felt as if he'd betrayed her, even though in truth, she was the one who'd screwed him over.

"Brit's fine," Marcus said. "But that's not what you're really asking, is it?"

"You're going to make me say it?" Logan bit out, irritation making him sound gruff. Why the hell did this all have to be so hard? Give him a straight out firefight over trying to figure out the ins and outs of a damned relationship any day. At least in a fight he knew where he stood.

"Yeah, I kinda like the idea of you scrambling."

"Fine. How is Ginny?"

"I don't actually know firsthand." Disappointment swept through him. God, this was ridiculous. "But," Marcus lifted up a hand, "Brit talked to her. And if it matters at all, I think the two of them are friends again. Or at least they're going to try. Brit's forgiven Ginny for what happened with her dad."

Logan tightened a fist thinking how much he'd enjoy plowing it right into the sanctimonious face of that son-of-a-bitch senator.

"My sentiments exactly," Marcus nodded, his eyes on Logan's fist. "But that isn't going to help anything. Anyway, Brit told Ginny that it wasn't a date. That we'd kinda roped you into it."

"Kinda?" He ran his finger around the rim of his glass.

"Yeah, well, it seemed like a good idea at the time."

"It wasn't a bad idea. I'm just not ready to date someone else. I don't know that I ever will be."

"Jesus, you really do have it bad."

"I do. And I'm not sure what the hell I should do about it."

"Not like you to take the coward's way out."

"What the hell are you talking about?" Logan frowned.

"Just that it's not like you not to face your troubles head on. Whatever is between you and Ginny, you're not going to work it out until you at least face the woman and talk about it."

"My sentiments exactly, Marcus." Sonya Murphy walked over to the bar with his burger and fries. "I always knew you had good sense."

"You always thought I got Logan in trouble."

"Don't be silly, son. I knew it was Logan all the time." She smiled and headed back to the kitchen.

Marcus sobered. "I'm not wrong, you know."

Logan stared down into the amber liquid in his glass. "I know. It's just hard."

"Nothing good is ever easy." Marcus popped a french fry into his mouth as the door opened and Brittany rushed inside.

"Oh, thank God you're here," Brittany said, coming to a full stop in front of them. She was breathing hard, her hand to her chest.

"What's wrong?" Marcus leapt out of his seat, reaching for her.

"Nothing. At least I don't think so. But I thought Logan should know."

"Know what?" Logan frowned, pulling to his feet, too.

"Ginny just went into labor."

"But isn't that early?" His heart started pounding, sweat breaking out on his forehead; if the baby didn't make it, Ginny would never be the same. She loved her child. That much he was certain of.

"Babies come when they're ready, I guess. Mallory said something about the senator. I think they had a fight."

"That slimy bastard. Just wait until I get my hands on him." Logan pushed away from the bar, anger crashing through him.

Marcus held out an arm, stopping his forward momentum. "Hold on a second. I know you're pissed. And I don't blame you. Hell, I'll help you take the son of a bitch out. But right now, the important thing is Ginny."

Logan ran a hand through his hair, his emotions threatening to unman him. "You're right. Where is she? At the hospital?"

"Yeah, Marisol and Ian took her."

Logan started to move again. "Then I need to get there. I need to be with her." In his frantic haste, he almost collided with his brother coming through the door.

"Whoa, where's the fire?" Dillon asked.

"It's Ginny," Logan said, feeling around in his pockets. "She's in labor. Where the fuck are my keys?"

"Easy, dude," Marcus said. "I'll drive. You're not in any state to do it."

Logan nodded.

"Wait," Dillon said, staring down at a text on his phone.

"What? Now you don't want me to be with her?" Logan asked, his impatience making him want to deck his brother, but something in Dillon's expression made him hold the thought.

"No." Dillon shook his head, still reading. "I think you need to go now. But I think Brittany should take you."

"Why wouldn't I go with them?" Marcus asked, his brows drawing together in a frown.

"Because I just got a call for a domestic disturbance. At your house."

Chapter 4

Dakota Alvarez jerked from sleep with a start, sitting up in her bed, trying to figure out what had awoken her. Sunlight slanted across the duvet and a glance through the window indicated that morning was waning, if not gone already. She'd stayed out way too late last night. Drinking in a nearby honky-tonk, trying to forget about the misery that was her life, at least a few hours.

A couple of guys had bought her beers, one of them wanting to take her home. But she'd had enough of men—at least for now. Unbidden thoughts of Patrick Murphy filled her head. He'd been flirting with her the other day at the Bluebonnet. She was certain of it. What she was less certain of was whether she wanted to do anything about it. Patrick wasn't the kind of guy a girl had a fling with. And as close as he was with his family, he most definitely wasn't going to be her ticket out of this town.

Then again, maybe she didn't need a man to free her. Maybe she was capable of doing it herself. She glanced across the room at the letter lying on top of the desk. Her friend Amanda Graceson had written with an invitation to visit. Amanda been Dakota's best friend when they were kids. Not so much as they'd grown older. Dakota's wild ways hadn't exactly been in tune with Amanda's more sedate way of doing things.

Actually, Amanda's mother had held the firm belief that Alvarezes and Gracesons were not meant to comingle. The Gracesons only falling slightly lower on the social ladder than the Rushes. Still, she and Amanda shared a past. And Amanda had an apartment in College Station where she attended college. Maybe it wouldn't hurt to consider a little time away.

Something in the next room shattered, and then the wall reverberated as something hit—hard.

Dakota frowned, jumping out of bed and dragging on a pair of jeans. A part of her wanted to run the other direction. Away from whatever her mother had done to upset her father. But another part of her, the part that had been through hell over the past months, felt a tiny frisson of something that might be concern.

Man, Patrick was getting to her in a big way.

Another crash was followed by what sounded like a sob.

Dakota squared her shoulders as she walked into the living room, but nothing she could have done could possibly have prepared her for what she found. The room was in shambles. Lamps overturned, a chair on its side—a hole in one of the walls. Her father was standing over her mother, his fist raised, his eyes wild. Her mother had her hands lifted, as if somehow she could ward off the blow.

The world seemed to switch to slow motion, her father's fist slamming into her mother, her mother's head whipping back with the force of the blow, her body hitting hard against the wall.

"Stupid bitch," her father was saying. "That'll teach you to whore around on me." He kicked her hard, and suddenly anger cut through Dakota's terror.

"Daddy, stop it. You're really hurting her."

Hector swung around, his gaze full of fire. "Get the hell out of here. This is between me and your mother."

She froze, looking at her father's angry face, and her mother sprawled on the floor against the wall. Patrick's words at the diner echoed in her head. *Somewhere deep down you would definitely know it.* "Leave her alone, Daddy."

"I'll do with her as I please. She's mine," Hector snarled and this time Dakota was reminded of the senator—the night in his cabin when he'd taken her over a table.

With courage she hadn't known she possessed, she stepped between her father and her mother. "I mean it, Daddy. Stand back."

"Stupid little girl, get out of my way," he said, his fist swinging before she even had time to realize what was happening.

The blow sent her reeling backward, her head slamming into the wall even as her face exploded with pain. The world wobbled and she blinked, trying to focus, her heart pounding as she looked up at her father. He didn't even look sorry. Just angry and annoyed.

He reached for her again, his fingers clamping on her arms, jerking her upward. "You think you're so high and mighty. But you're no better than your mother—spreading your legs for any man who walks by. You're both whores. And you deserve everything you're going to get." He shook her hard, her teeth rattling in her head, and Dakota had never in her life been so afraid.

He raised his hand—but the blow never came, her mother pushing herself between Dakota and Hector, her father's fist slamming into her mother again as Joanne tried to protect her daughter.

Tears sprang to Dakota's eyes as Joanne faced Hector. Not weak and useless but strong and brave. A mother defending her child.

"You leave Dakota out of this, Hector," Joanne hissed, blood dripping from the corner of her mouth, her eye almost swollen shut. "This is between you and me." She shifted slightly, drawing Hector away from Dakota. "Sweetie, I want you to leave."

"No," Dakota shook her head, frantically looking around her for some kind of weapon. "I'm not leaving without you."

"Dakota, go." Her mother's voice was strained, but firm. And a part of Dakota wanted to obey, but before she could decide what to do, Hector lunged at Joanne, pulling a gun from behind his back.

"Daddy, no," she screamed as he squeezed her mother's throat and pointed the gun at Joanne's head.

Behind her the door crashed open and Marcus threw himself across the room at his father. He hit him with a sickening thud, Joanne scrambling backward as she was thrown to the floor. Dakota watched terrified as the two men struggled for control of the gun, and then suddenly the sharp report of a gunshot filled the living room. Marcus fell backward, and Dakota heard somebody scream. Then her father had her mother in a chokehold again.

"Stand back," he yelled. "I'll kill her right here. Right now."

Dakota made a move to go to her brother, but Hector shifted toward her, the muzzle of the gun leveled at her now. "Leave him be. He doesn't deserve your concern. The sniveling bastard. Should have drowned him when he was a kid."

"Daddy, please," she said, her voice quaking so hard the words hardly came out at all. "Let Momma go. Put the gun down."

"And what? Wait for the sheriff to shoot me?" He tipped his head at Dillon, who was standing in the doorway, his weapon drawn.

"Put it down, Hector. You don't want to kill your daughter. Or your wife."

"Always trying to tell me what I feel." He waved the gun in the air, and Dakota drew a shaky breath. "You've always thought you were so much better than me. But remember that she chose me. Not you. Me. She's mine. And I'm damn sure not going to surrender her to the likes of you." He tightened his hold on Joanne, her eyes going wide as she struggled to breathe.

Behind Hector, Marcus was coming around.

Dakota started to move toward him, but he shook his head, lifting a finger to his lips. Hector had no idea he was conscious. With a tiny nod, she swallowed and lifted her chin, determined to pull her father's attention away from her brother. "Daddy, you need to let her go. Sheriff Murphy is right. This isn't going to end well for any of us."

"You going to stop me, baby girl?" Hector taunted. "Trust me, if I'm going down, I'm going to take your whore of a mother with me."

The tears spilled hot against Dakota's cheeks as she saw for the first time what her father truly was. "Momma," she whispered, her gaze colliding with her mother's. "I'm so sorry."

"Fine time to grow a conscience." Hector sneered. "But don't you think it's a little too late? Once a tramp, always a tramp."

Hector jerked Joanne backward, the gun lowering slightly as he shifted. Seeing the chance, Marcus dove for their mother, the momentum jerking Joanne free. Hector growled and lifted the gun, pointing it at Dakota. Shock and horror held her frozen in place. She heard her mother scream her name and then the sound of another gunshot.

Hector stood for a moment, hatred contorting his face as he stared at her, and then he fell.

Dillon Murphy lowered his weapon, his face filled with anguish as his gaze found Joanne. There was so much love reflected there, it almost hurt Dakota to see it. Her mother was checking Marcus for injury. His arm was bloody, but other than that he appeared to be whole. His eyes met hers across the room, and he nodded once, then turned his attention back to their mother.

Dakota sucked in a ragged breath and looked down at her father's sightless eyes. She didn't belong here. She wasn't one of the good guys. She'd been so stupid and so wrong. And so, so, so many other things.

With a last glance at her family, she turned and did the only thing she really did well—run away.

* * * *

Kristin Douglas sat on a back pew in her brother's church. Sunlight streamed through the stained-glass windows casting colored patterns across the wood-planked floor. It was quiet, with no one about, peaceful in a way Kristin hadn't felt in a really long time. Despite all the pain in their childhood, her brother's faith had always been his salvation. He'd never doubted that there was a higher power out there and that it would somehow always manage to make things right.

Kristin wished she could believe. But it wasn't easy for her. Not like it was with Bryce. Although lately, even his faith had been shaken. Danny hadn't been part of her brother's plan for a perfect family. But slowly, with Tara's help, Bryce was starting to understand that sometimes happiness came in imperfect packages. And that happy families took a lot of work.

All relationships took a lot of work.

And sometimes a relationship turned out to be something other than what it had promised to be. She blew out a sigh, wondering when she'd turned so cynical. Maybe when she'd decided to carry on an affair with a married man. The funny thing about it was that she'd never have thought herself the type. She'd hated her mother for all the men she'd dragged through their young lives. Many of them married.

And here she was doing the same.

Except that it wasn't like that. She loved Travis. For better or worse—mostly worse. Because she hated the fact that she was hurting Celeste. It was easy to pretend that she didn't care about the woman. Or to tell herself that Celeste had made her own bed. But the truth was even if she had, it didn't negate the fact that Kristin was taking what wasn't hers.

She dipped her head, the smell of candle wax and floor polish giving her a strange kind of comfort. At least here, in her brother's house of worship, for an all too brief moment, she felt at peace.

"Hey, big sister, I didn't expect to see you here this morning. Did I forget a meeting?" Despite the unusual heat, Bryce looked crisp and professional in his khakis and button down.

"No meeting," she smiled, realizing for the millionth time how lucky she was to have him in her life. "Just wanted a quiet place to do some thinking."

"I don't think there's a better place in Storm," he agreed,

settling down on the pew next to her. "Anything in particular got you down? Or just life in general?"

"I guess, I was just wondering how I managed to wind up where I am. I mean, one minute you have a plan for your life and the next you realize you've taken a wrong turn somewhere along the way and now you're hopelessly lost." She hadn't meant to be so honest, but there was something so comforting about the quiet and her brother.

"I don't think it's ever hopeless, Kristin. Maybe you just got off course a little. Or maybe you just need to stop and look around and then you'll realize you're not lost at all."

"But how can you, of all people, say that?" Her gaze moved to meet her brother's.

"I don't have all the answers. I can't say with any surety what's black and what's white. There are so many different degrees. And so many nuances that go undefined. I just have to trust my heart. And my God. And follow His guidelines to the best of my ability. But the bottom line is that I'm human and so I'm going to screw up. Look what happened with Danny. I almost lost my marriage and my son because I was too caught up in the idea of a perfect family."

"But you didn't lose them. And you realized that you were making a mistake," Kristin said.

"I realized what I stood to lose. That's really what it's all about. For me, it's you and Tara and Carol and Danny. You're everything to me. And I can't let anything else stand in the way of that. Especially not my own elevated notions of what is supposed to be."

"But what if you know you're doing something wrong, but you also know you're doing it for the right reasons? Which doesn't make any sense at all, I know." She leaned back, letting her gaze move to the large wooden cross over the altar. "In theory it seems so cut and dried. Do that, don't do this. But in reality, it's so messy."

"Shades of gray," Bryce nodded. "I think the key is to be true to yourself, Kristin. And as I said, to protect the people you love."

"Except that's tricky when the person you love is the reason you're hurting others."

"Look," Bryce said, turning to face her, "you know I can't condone adultery. But I also know that we can't help who we love."

"Which leaves me in a hole I can't possibly get out of. Admittedly a hole I dug for myself, but nevertheless a hole. Bryce, I can't go on like this. Even loving him the way I do. It's eating me up inside. When we're together I'm so happy. But when we're apart, I feel dirty. And ugly. Like part of me is withering inside."

"Oh, sis, I hate that you're going through this. In fact, I'm not sure that I don't hate him for putting you in this position. But I also know that if he truly loves you, then ultimately, this will all turn out alright."

"You make it sound so simple."

"Hey, that's my job." He smiled, and then sobered. "But seriously, I'm not trying to make light of a very complicated situation. There are so many variables at play. But you need to be sure of more than just your feelings for him, Kristin. You have to be sure of his feelings for you. Because if he doesn't love you the way you love him, then he doesn't deserve you. And that much, at least, I'm certain of."

Kristin nodded, her eyes filling with tears. "I love you, Bryce."

"And I love you. And so do Tara and the kids. You have a family, Kristin. And no matter what happens, we stand behind you. Don't ever forget that. It's you and me, kid. Always." He squeezed her hand then pushed to his feet. "I'm here if you need me. But in the meantime, I've got a sermon to write."

She watched as her brother walked through the door leading to his office, and then slowly pushed to her feet. Nothing was going to be solved in the moment. And she couldn't hide in her brother's church forever.

She walked through the vestibule and out into the sunshine of the square.

"Kristin?" Her heart beat faster as she took in his broad

shoulders and lined face.

"Is your brother around?" Travis asked, shooting a glance at the doors to the church.

"He's in his office."

Travis chewed on his lower lip for a second and then grabbed her arm, pulling her into the shelter of the church's rose garden chapel.

"We need to talk," he said without preamble, and Kristin felt a shiver of worry.

"We do? About what?"

Travis looked around furtively, then closed the distance between them, taking Kristin's hands. "I signed divorce papers today."

Her gut clenched and her heart twisted. He'd actually done it. "Today? You signed them today?"

"Yeah." He nodded. "This morning, actually."

Her heart was threatening to break right out of her chest. "I didn't realize...I mean, you said you were going to ask her, but...I had no idea that you—"

"Actually, I didn't. Celeste did. Apparently she had the papers drawn up before Jacob died."

"Before..." Kristin shook her head, trying to align the facts of what was happening. "So Celeste decided to leave you."

"Well, it doesn't matter who initiated it," his smile was cautious. "The point is, I'm a free man."

"But why did she want a divorce?" Kristin asked, her heart plummeting.

"She says she doesn't love me anymore." There was hurt in his eyes. Pain that wasn't in tune with the supposed relief he was trying to convey.

"Did she know about us, Travis?"

He looked down at his hands, the silence stretching between them for a moment, then he lifted his head and shrugged. "Yeah. She knew. Apparently since the beginning."

"But she never gave you the papers." Kristin suddenly felt as if she'd committed an unpardonable sin. Celeste had been through so much.

"No. Jacob died, and she couldn't face it. Couldn't face me, truth be told."

"And now?"

"Now she's ready to get on with her life. And she doesn't want me to be a part of it. She even said she wished us well."

"You and me." She should be feeling ecstatic but instead she felt confused. Let down, somehow. He hadn't asked Celeste for a divorce. He hadn't chosen her. He hadn't done anything except lose his wife and come straight to the woman he no doubt expected to pick up the pieces. Or worse, the woman he expected to console him physically. Hadn't that always been the way with Travis? Expecting her to be at his beck and call?

"So you had no idea this was coming?"

"No, it came out of the blue. You could have knocked me over with a feather. I had no idea she was upset about me. Or that she even knew about us."

"So this all came from Celeste. You had no intention of doing anything yourself." Suddenly everything seemed crystal clear, and she wasn't certain she liked the picture.

"I told you before, I thought she was too fragile. I didn't want to hurt her any more than I already had."

It was always about Celeste.

"Well, I'm sorry she's left you." She pulled her hands free.

He frowned, clearly confused. "But I thought you'd be happy. Now we can be together."

"And get married and start a family?" she said, not certain where the words were coming from, but knowing that they had to be said.

He blanched. "I've got kids already, Kristin. You know I don't want any more. And hey, there's no need to rush into marriage. I mean, I only just got out of this one."

She nodded, surprised her heart hadn't spilt out bleeding onto the floor. And then she saw the light from the windows again, this time the colors dancing across the garden path, their beauty an unexpected source of strength.

"Of course. I totally understand. And I wish you the best of luck with your new life."

"But Kristin…"

She took one last look at the man she'd thought she loved, then turned and walked away. In the doorway at the front of the church, her brother stood waiting.

Chapter 5

"How are you feeling?" Marisol asked as she handed Ginny a cup of water.

Monitors beeped all around her as she sat propped up in the hospital bed. For the moment at least, everything was calm. Ginny's obstetrician had verified that she was indeed in labor, but Little Bit didn't appear to be in any great hurry to make an entrance.

Ginny sipped her water, one hand resting protectively on her stomach. "I'm fine. A lot calmer now that we're here and settled in. But to be honest, I still keep expecting the senator to come bursting through those doors with a fleet of lawyers."

"Let him try it," Marisol said, eyes narrowing in anger. "Ian's out there, which means he'll have to get through him first."

"Ian's a good guy." Ginny said, lips curling in a smile. "Luis said you guys were kissing." Her sister deserved some happiness.

"It was just a peck. A congratulatory kiss. Ian bought land for Marcus's ranch." Marisol actually blushed.

"What about Patrick?" It had been pretty obvious that any interest Marisol had had in Patrick exited stage left when Ian entered the picture, but Ginny hadn't had the chance to ask her sister about it.

"We're good, I think."

"I'm glad to hear it. I was a little worried that you'd called things off with him because of Logan. Or that he'd called things off with you."

"No. Not at all. The truth is we were never really more than just good friends. We were both just ready for something more and so I think we tried to make it happen."

"You mean Patrick tried."

"Yeah, and I hid behind you and Luis. But anyway, we're okay. And I'm determined not to hide anymore."

"With Ian."

"Maybe, I don't know." A shadow crossed her sister's face. "He's leaving, Ginny. Going back to Montana. I don't want to let myself hope for more than he's offering. You know?"

"I do." Ginny nodded, wincing a little as a contraction hit her. "But you deserve to be happy. If not with Ian, than with someone."

"Well, right now there are more important things to be thinking about than Ian Briggs. You're about to have a baby. And the two of you are still my first priority."

"And I love you for that. But Little Bit and I are going to be okay. Whatever happens. Whoever the father turns out to be, we're going to be okay."

"Yeah, well, I'll be there to help make sure of that." Her sister squeezed her hand, and then set the cup back on the bedside table. "How are the contractions?"

"Not too bad actually. But I'm pretty certain this is just the warm-up round. The doctor said it would probably be a while before things really kick in."

"Good thing there are epidurals. I can't imagine why anyone would want to—" Marisol broke off as raised voices carried through the partially open hospital room door.

"I don't care what the rules say," an angry masculine voice was saying. "I'm going in to see her."

"I'm sorry, but only family is allowed. And you're not family," an equally strident voice responded.

There was the sound of a scuffle and then the door flew all the way open. Logan pushed into the room, breathing heavily, his gaze moving across the room to collide with Ginny's. "Are you and Little Bit okay?"

"We're fine," Ginny choked out, the beeping on the monitor speeding up as her heart rate ratcheted upward.

"What are you doing here?" Marisol asked, coming to her feet, looking every inch the protective momma.

"I need to talk to Ginny." Logan looked from Ginny to Marisol and then back to Ginny again. "Please, Ginny. Just let me stay for a few minutes."

Ginny swallowed, her hands going clammy. She'd dreamed of this moment. Of him coming to her. Only in her dreams she hadn't been lying in a hospital bed in labor. Hardly the stuff of romantic fantasy. And yet, nothing about their time together had been anything close to normal, and the point was that he was here.

"Marisol," she said, her voice still sounding funny, "can you give us a moment?"

Her sister reached out to smooth Ginny's hair. "You sure you'll be all right?"

She nodded, her heart doing little flip-flops. Logan moved to the side of the bed as Marisol left the room—pausing for a moment at the door to watch them both.

"I'll be fine," Ginny said, hoping she was telling the truth.

And then it was just the two of them, Logan's hot gaze seeming to devour her. Ginny struggled to breathe and for a moment they just looked at each other in silence. Then Logan dropped into the chair by her bed and took her hand.

"Oh, God, Ginny, I was scared to death. When I heard that you'd had a confrontation with the senator, I almost lost my mind. The only reason the bastard is still walking around is because I needed to check on you first. To make sure you were okay."

"We're okay," she said, patting her belly.

"Truly?" he asked, his fingers tightening on hers.

"Yes." She nodded, then shrugged, trying to appear calm. "I'll admit the senator scared me a little. And the doctor thinks that the stress might have sped things along. But he says it's all going to be fine. Little Bit is strong. And so am I." She didn't feel particularly strong, but she wasn't about to let him know how frightened she'd really been.

"Well, there's no way that man is getting his claws into your baby."

Ginny gave him a small smile, loving the feel of his fingers twined with hers. God, she'd give anything to have him be a part of her life again. "I've got a lot of amazing people in my corner. If nothing else, we won't make it easy on him."

"You're the bravest woman I know," Logan said, his eyes flashing with an emotion she was almost afraid to try and identify.

"No. I'm not." She shook her head, fighting tears. "If I was, I'd have told the truth about the baby from the beginning. I'd never have lied to Celeste and to my family. And most importantly, I'd never have lied to you."

"You were caught off guard. I get that. And you did what you thought was best in the moment. If I learned anything at all when I was in Afghanistan, it's that in a crisis the moment is really all you've got. A split second to make a decision that could potentially affect you for the rest of your life. When you woke up and learned that Jacob was dead and that you were pregnant, you did what you needed to do to protect your child. I can't pretend the lie didn't hurt me. It did. But that doesn't mean I can't understand why you did it."

"I never meant to hurt anyone," she said, the tears flowing now. "But I did. And worst of all, I hurt you—the most important person in my life. If I could take it back… If I could do it all over again…"

He reached over to wipe away her tears. "Maybe what's more important is that instead of looking back, we try to move forward."

"We?" Ginny asked, hope blooming deep inside her.

"Yeah," he said, leaning over to kiss her. "You and me." He laid his big hand across her swollen belly. "And Little Bit. If you guys will have me. I've been such an ass, Ginny."

"No." She shook her head, covering his hand with hers. "You had every right to be upset. To walk away. I don't blame you at all. I just wanted...I just wanted us to be together."

"I shouldn't have been so judgmental. I should have been able to understand. To forgive you. It's just that I was so hurt. And angry. And, well, I got lost in all of that. I wanted to come to you so many times, but then I'd just get pissed all over again."

"And now?"

"Now I just want to be with you."

"Because of the baby?" She swallowed, putting her fears front and center. If they were going to move forward, she was determined to be nothing less than honest. "I don't need your pity."

"God, Ginny, I don't pity you. I already said how brave I think you are and how much I admire your strength. But I know better than most that you can't do it all on your own. I think we're better off together. You're the woman I want to spend my life with. No matter what baggage comes along with you." His warm hand smoothed the skin across her stomach. "And I don't mean Little Bit."

She shivered, thinking of the senator. "It isn't going to be easy. But if he comes at me, I'm going to fight him."

"And if you'll let me, I'll be right there with you. I won't let him hurt you again. I don't know what happened. Or why you were with him. I meant what I said; that's all in the past. But the bottom line here is that the son of a bitch is a habitual cheater who preys on young, innocent women, and there's no way he comes out a winner after doing that."

Ginny held Logan's gaze for a moment, chewing on her lower lip. "The baby could still be Jacob's."

"I hope it is. For both of your sakes. But it doesn't matter to me. All that matters to me is that Little Bit is yours. And that I love you. And as long as you'll have me, I want a place in your life."

"You love me?" The words came out on a stutter, joy flooding through Ginny's entire being.

"I do. And I want to be a family."

As if the baby heard Logan's words, a little foot connected with his hand. Logan's eyes widened and he grinned. "I think

Little Bit agrees. Which places the ball squarely in your court. Because this isn't just about me. It's about you. It's about us. So what do you want, Ginny?"

"You," she said, lifting a hand to cup his face. "I want you. I love you. I need you." Their gazes met and held, and then Logan covered her lips with his, his kiss a promise—a covenant.

And suddenly Ginny felt as if anything were possible.

* * * *

Marisol stood at the coffee machine trying to get control of her rioting emotions. Logan was in with Ginny and a part of her was elated, but another part of her was terrified. She wanted her sister to be happy. To have that elusive happy ending. But she didn't want to see her hurt. And there was potential for either of those things where Logan Murphy was concerned.

"Ginny all right?" A deep voice asked. Talk about potential for disaster. Marisol's breath hitched as she turned to face Ian, eyes dark with worry.

"She's fine. Logan is in there with her. I felt like a third wheel." She offered a shaky smile. "I figured it was better to leave them alone."

"Let them find their own way. It isn't always easy to do that." His expression indicated he knew only too well how difficult that was.

"You're thinking of Marcus."

"I am. He's been through a lot."

"I heard what happened. I can't even imagine."

"I know. And of course Marcus is trying to be strong for his sisters and his mother."

"He'll need you now more than ever."

"And I'll be here for him."

Marisol was embarrassed by the little trill of joy that blossomed deep inside her. "He's lucky to have you."

"I don't suppose with everything that's going on we're going to be able to have that dinner tonight." Ian tilted his head to one side, his steady gaze making her feel hot inside.

"I guess not."

"Well, then we'll just have to reschedule it. There's all the time in the world." He stepped closer, taking both of her hands in his.

"But what about Montana? You live in Montana."

"Not anymore." He shook his head. "From here on out, I'm living in Storm. Even rented an apartment over on Ash. I can manage the Montana ranch from here. Make a few trips a year as needed. It's all good."

"Marcus must be over the moon. Seeing all that's happened and how close you are, I can understand why you'd want to stay."

"He's not the only reason I'm staying, Marisol," he said, his breath caressing her cheek. "I hope I haven't misread things." His gaze darkened as he frowned. "I know you had a thing with Patrick Murphy. But I'd hoped—"

"Patrick and I aren't together," she interrupted, her heart pounding so loudly she figured everyone in the hospital could probably hear it. "We've only ever been just friends really." It was a condensed version but basically the truth.

His fingers tightened on hers. "Well, then, as I was saying, I'd hoped that maybe there might be a chance for you and me. I know we haven't really talked about this, but since the first moment I laid eyes on you, I knew you were special. And I haven't been able to get you out of my head for a moment since."

He moved forward, and God help her, right here in front of anyone who might be passing by, she closed her eyes and leaned into him, relishing the exquisite moment when he crushed his lips against hers.

Maybe Ginny wasn't the only one who deserved a happy ending.

* * * *

Dakota sat huddled beneath the giant live oak hanging out over the placid water of the lake. The quiet inlet had been a favorite place since she'd been old enough to ride a bike, the grassy knoll providing escape from the things that hurt her.

Hugging her knees, she struggled to breathe, the tears still coming fast and hard. She hardly remembered leaving her house and driving here, her head stuck on an endless visual loop of her father beating her mother, shooting Marcus—aiming the gun at her.

She rubbed a hand against her bruised cheek, trying to make sense of it all. She'd always believed her father loved her. That he accepted her for who she was. But he'd called her a tramp. Implied worse. And the disgust in his eyes. She shuddered and wiped at her tears, as if somehow she would erase the memory as well.

She'd been so stupid. So blind. She'd followed her father like some kind of puppy. Waiting for his praise, begging for his approval. And all the time he'd been playing her. Making her believe in him. Making her hate her mother. Shame washed through her—hot and heavy. When Hector had come at her, her mother had stepped between them. Fearlessly trying to protect Dakota.

That was love. Not the syrupy crap her father served up. She'd been so needy and desperate she'd believed him. Believed in him. Just like she'd believed in the senator. But they'd both used her. Used her desire to be loved and taken what they wanted. God, what had she done? Marcus had tried to tell her. Mallory had tried to tell her. Even Patrick had tried. And she hadn't listened. She hadn't wanted to see the truth. She'd been too locked in her own little world to see what was happening right in front of her nose.

Her father had been abusing her mother. And her mother had taken it to protect her children. To protect Dakota. To secure her stupid fantasy world. She'd never meant anything to anyone that she'd believed in. And the people who had loved her, she'd shoved away with scorn.

What the hell was she supposed to do now?

She stared out at the still waters of the lake. It was beautiful, the air cooling as evening set in, the colors of the sky reflected in the ripples below. Somewhere in the distance she could hear the harsh cry of a blue jay as the wind whispered through the leaves of the trees.

She rested her chin on her knees and fought to calm her racing heart. There'd been blood everywhere. On the walls and the floor. On Marcus and her mother and her father. Hector had looked so surprised, an angry hatred twisting his face into a caricature, something from a book or a movie. It was as if the father she'd believed in had morphed into another man.

But deep in her heart she knew that in truth, for the first time she'd seen the real Hector Alvarez. Seen who he truly was. Who he had always been. And more frightening than even that, she'd seen a vision of what she might become. She'd let hatred and jealousy eat at her life. She'd blamed everyone for her problems. Her mother. Ginny. Even the senator.

It would be so easy now to just run farther away. To leave them all behind. To never see anyone in Storm again. End the chapter. Close the book. Run. But even as she had the thought, she knew she couldn't do it. Not if she wanted to survive. If she wanted to change. At least not without seeing her mom. Without facing her family. Patrick was right; deep down, she had known the truth. She just hadn't been willing to face it.

"Dakota?"

She turned, eyes going wide. Patrick strode across the meadow toward her as if she'd conjured him from somewhere inside her mind.

"Are you okay? I've been looking everywhere for you." He knelt down beside her, his hands gentle as he turned her face into the light. "That's quite a shiner."

She stiffened at his touch. "It's nothing compared to my mother. How did you know I was here?"

"Marcus said this is where you come when you're upset."

She was surprised that he knew. They'd never been that close, she and Marcus. Always circling each other, trying to avoid the landmines that surrounded her family. He'd tried to help her. But she'd always pushed him away. And then it had been his turn to run. And she'd hated him for escaping, never understanding that there had been something real to run from.

"I wasn't going to come here at all. I was heading for College Station. Amanda Graceson asked me to come and I figured it would be better for everyone if I just left. But then I couldn't somehow. I don't know, I felt guilty, I guess. So I came here."

"It's a beautiful place," he said, looking out across the lake and meadow, seemingly content to just sit with her here.

She sucked in a breath, lifting her gaze to Patrick's, the tender concern reflected there almost her undoing. "My mother?" The words came out on a whisper, and Dakota realized she was afraid of his answer.

"She's in the hospital. She's pretty banged up. But the doc said she'll be okay."

Dakota nodded, the reel still playing in her head. "And my father?"

Patrick released a long puff of air. "He's dead, Dakota."

She nodded. She'd already known it, of course, but somehow Patrick saying the words was what made it seem true.

"Dillon didn't have a choice." His words were careful, as if he was afraid she'd argue. But there was no doubt. If Dillon hadn't fired, she'd be dead. Or her mother. Or her brother. Or maybe all of them. Hector had been beyond any kind of reasoning. He'd been so filled with his own version of reality that he'd lost his grip on sanity.

"I know." She sighed, turning to watch as a bird skimmed across the top of the water. "He did what he had to. And he probably saved our lives. Daddy had a gun. And I know he would have used it."

"Dakota, I'm so sorry."

"For what? You didn't make my family so dysfunctional. My father did that. And me. I'm just like him, you know? So full of hatred and anger."

"But you don't have to be."

"How can I be anything else? I've fucked my life up so royally. I mean, first with the senator, and then with Ginny and the announcement and all the rest. I screwed over people who cared about me. And I believed in people who didn't. What kind of person does that make me?"

"Human," Patrick said, reaching for her hand. "It makes you human."

"But how can they ever forgive me? How can I forgive myself? I've made so many mistakes, Patrick." She laid her cheek against her knee, ignoring the pain as she brushed against her bruises. "I've hurt so many people."

"My grandfather always says that the only way to go forward is to begin as you mean to go on."

"What does that mean?"

"It means you have to decide the kind of person you are. And if you truly want to change, then you have to take the first step."

"I don't know how."

"Sure you do," he said, tipping her chin up again, forcing her to meet his gaze. "It's there inside you, Dakota. Beneath the fear and anger, there's the real you. And I think if you'd give her a chance, you might even like her."

"Do you always see the good in really awful people?" she asked, losing herself in the pale blue of his eyes.

"Only when I know there's a good heart in there somewhere." His smile stole her breath away as he leaned in to kiss her. For a minute the world shrank until it contained just the two of them, his warmth promising things she'd never believed in. And then a mockingbird scolded from the tree above, the moment broken.

He pushed to his feet and held out his hand. "Come on. I'll take you to your mother."

For a moment fear held her immobile, and then she squared her shoulders and placed her fingers in his. And as he pulled her to her feet, Dakota wondered if people really did get second chances. Because God knew she wanted one.

Chapter 6

"We don't have to walk in together," Mary Louise Prager said as she looked across the yard toward the gathering at the Johnsons'.

The entire family was present for an impromptu barbeque to celebrate Anna Mae and Chase's engagement. Well, both families. Hers and Tate's. Which meant that Mary Louise had to go. But she didn't have to show up on Tate's arm.

"Are you saying you don't want to be seen with me?" he asked, the teasing light in his eyes helping to set her at ease.

"No, of course not. It's just that we haven't actually told anyone that we…that you and I…"

"That we're an item," he prompted, his grin growing wider. "Is that the word you're looking for?"

"Is that what we are?" In actuality, she hadn't been certain. True enough they'd been spending a lot of time together. Most of it in bed. But they hadn't actually gone on any official dates, which meant she hadn't been sure.

Tate turned her to face him, his expression growing serious. "Mary Louise, as far as I am concerned, we are most definitely together. In every sense of the word. So unless you have a problem with that, I don't see why we shouldn't use this barbeque as the perfect opportunity to show our families that Chase and Anna Mae aren't the only ones who are happy."

"But what about Hannah?" she asked, knowing she was being stubborn.

"I don't want Hannah," he said, dipping his head to kiss the end of her nose. "I want you."

Mary Louise smiled up into his eyes. "And I want you right back. So let's go to the party." He slid an arm around her and they walked across the lawn to where everyone was gathered.

"Mary Louise, Tate," Rita Mae called when she saw them, "I was wondering when the two of you would get here." Her eyes twinkled with delight as she took in Tate's possessive hold. "Looks like life has been treating you all well."

"Indeed it has, Rita Mae," Tate said. "Your niece has been taking good care of me."

"Well, someone has to do it." Mary Louise smiled and accepted a beer from Tate's father, Zeke.

"Welcome, Mary Louise. I hope my oldest son has been behaving himself."

It seemed everyone was more in the know than she'd realized. She supposed she shouldn't have been surprised. After all, this was Storm, where everybody knew everybody's business. Across the way she could see her aunt Anna Mae glowing beside Chase.

"She looks so happy."

"Some things are just meant to be, I guess," Zeke said as Alice came to stand beside him.

"Now that everyone is here, we need to get the meat on, Zeke," she scolded. "Hungry people and all that."

"Yes, ma'am. I live to serve." Zeke winked at them and followed his wife toward a group of grills and smokers set off from the back patio.

"And that, sweetheart," Tate said, "is the picture of a perfect marriage."

"What?" Mary Louise laughed. "Your mom says jump and your dad says how high?"

"Nah, just her needing him and him making her happy." He pulled her closer as Tucker and Hannah walked up, the two of them looking delighted and uncomfortable all at the same time.

"Hey, bro, glad you could make it," Tucker said with a hesitant grin. Things between Tate and his brother weren't perfect by a long shot, but they were better. And Mary Louise was glad to see Tate returning Tucker's smile.

"Wouldn't have missed it for the world," Tate replied. "Looks like things are going well for the two of you." For a moment both men looked uncomfortable, and then Tate laughed, his arm sliding back around Mary Louise. "It isn't always easy to find the right woman," Tate continued. "But from where I'm standing, it's well worth the effort."

Tucker lifted his beer. "To happy endings."

They all clinked bottles and smiled. Then Hannah's phone buzzed and she excused herself while Tucker headed off to help his dad.

"That was really nice of you," Mary Louise said as they walked over toward where Tara and Bryce were holding court with their children.

Tate's warm gaze encompassed hers. "I meant every word." Her stomach fluttered and she felt her face growing hot again. Tate just grinned as they stopped in front of his sister's family.

Bryce was standing just beyond the stone wall that divided the patio from the rest of the yard, tossing a ball with Danny. Carol was trying to make a Hula-Hoop twirl around her hips, but was having no luck at all. Tara was laughing as she watched her daughter try.

"You have to get it twirling first and then move your hips," Mary Louise said, pulling away from Tate to demonstrate the motion.

Carol watched and then tried again, the hoop actually making a full revolution before it fell.

"You have to keep moving, sweetie," Tara said. The two women watched as Carol tried again, this time with almost two revolutions.

"You're getting it," Mary Louise encouraged. "You just have to keep trying."

"Ah, Carol, don't listen to them," Rita Mae said, striding over to where the little girl was still struggling. "I was the two-time Hula-Hoop champion of Storm High. Come with me, kid, I'll show you how it's done."

With a quick look at her mother, Carol danced off with Rita Mae, their two heads bent together as they discussed the fine art of hula-hooping.

"Well, that should be interesting," Tara commented as they watched the pair walk away.

"The blind leading the blind," Mary Louise said.

"You and my brother seem to be cozy these days." Tara waggled her eyebrows suggestively and Mary Louise felt herself growing bright red.

"We're seeing each other." God, even standing here in the middle of his family, she had a hard time believing it was true.

"I know. And from where I'm sitting, it looks like it might be getting serious."

"Would that be a bad thing?" Mary Louise asked hesitantly.

"Goodness, no," Tara said, reaching out to pull Mary Louise into a quick hug. "More like a miracle. Tate's needed someone like you in his life for the longest time."

"But he was with Hannah." It felt like just saying her name was going to jinx everything somehow.

"Like you said, *was*. And in case you haven't gotten the memo," Tara nodded over to where her brother Tucker and Hannah were talking with Tara's sister-in-law Kristin, "she's got it bad for my baby brother. So I'm thinking maybe things have worked out just the way they're supposed to have."

Mary Louise smiled, pushing aside her insecurities. "Well, I guess I can't argue with that."

"Argue with what?" Bryce asked, walking up behind Tara and dropping a kiss on the top of her head.

"Love," Tara replied, her eyes crinkling at the corners as she leaned back into her husband's arms.

"Here's to that," Zeke said, his deep voice carrying across the gathered crowd. "And on that note, I want to propose a toast to my big brother and the love of his life, Miss Anna Mae Prager. Here's wishing you both the very best."

Zeke lifted his beer bottle into the air, and everyone else followed suite. Chase gave a big whoop and twirled Anna Mae around in a circle.

"They look so happy," Tucker said, joining the group.

"I'm glad they found each other again," Tate agreed, slipping an arm around Mary Louise. "It gives a guy hope."

"Tucker," Hannah called, slipping her phone into her pocket as she walked toward them.

"Everything all right?" he asked, quickly stepping to her side.

"No." She shook her head, her eyes welling with tears. "It's my sister. She's in the hospital. And Hector...Hector is dead."

* * * *

Joanne slowly opened her eyes, recognizing the institutional white walls of Storm's hospital. For a moment, she struggled to remember why she was here, then reality hit with a speed that robbed her of breath.

Hector was dead.

She lay for a moment, letting the idea sink in.

Dead.

The man she'd once loved. The man she'd learned to fear. The man who'd destroyed her family. He was dead.

There should be horror or sadness or delight.

But instead she felt only relief. Blessed, blessed relief.

Slowly she sat up, trying to assess the damage. Her eye was almost swollen shut, and her cheek throbbed in agony. Her arm was in a splint and she could feel the pressure bandage around her ribs. She'd been lucky. Truly lucky. But her kids. Dear God, Marcus had almost been killed trying to rescue her. And Dakota...Dakota had seen it all. She'd watched as Hector died. She'd worshiped her father. Dear Lord, what had it cost her to witness his madness?

She tried to swing her feet around to the edge of the bed. She needed to find her children. But the world swung in a crazy circle and she swallowed against the rush of pain.

"Careful, Mom," Marcus said, striding through the door and across the room to slide a protective arm around her waist as he eased her back down onto the bed. "You need to be resting."

"But I need to check on Mallory and…"

"I'm right here, Momma." Mallory stood in the doorway, looking so young and lost.

"And Dakota?" Joanne lay back, looking to her oldest.

"Patrick Murphy is looking for her. They've become friends, and I figured she'd be more likely to talk to him than to me. So don't worry. He'll find her. What's important now is that you let us take care of you."

"I'm fine," she said as Mallory came to perch on the chair beside the bed. Marcus leaned back against the windowsill, crossing his arms over his chest as he watched them both. "Just a little bit banged up."

"A little bit?" Marcus's eyebrows rose. "You've got two broken ribs, a hairline fracture in your cheek, and your shoulder was dislocated. I'd say that qualifies as more than just a bit banged up."

"Marcus," Mallory chastised, going from kid to adult in a split second. Joanne shuddered with remorse. What had she done to her children? "She doesn't need your anger on top of everything else."

"I'm sorry." Marcus nodded, clearly struggling with his emotions. "I didn't mean to sound harsh. It's just that you're not okay. None of us are. We probably never will be completely. But the important thing here is that he's gone. And he can never hurt any of us again."

"Marcus is right," Mallory said in her too-adult voice. "We all survived. That's what matters."

"At least you weren't there," Joanne said, reaching over to brush a strand of hair from Mallory's face. "I'd have done anything to spare your brother and sister from what happened."

"But don't you see, Mom?" Marcus said. "That's partly why it was all so difficult. You never let us help you."

"How could I do that? I'm your mother. I'm supposed to protect you. I'm the fool who married Hector. I'm the fool who didn't have the strength to walk away. I couldn't let him hurt you, too." She watched her son, praying that he'd understand. That he'd forgive her.

"So you drove me away."

"No. But I let you go. Because I wanted you to live. I knew that if I let you stay, either Hector would kill you or you'd kill Hector. And neither of those options were acceptable. Either way you'd have to pay for my sins."

"But what about Dakota and Mallory?"

"Mom protected me," Mallory said, and Joanne felt a rush of love for her youngest. "Daddy never hit me. He never even tried. Mom never left us alone together. And he worshiped Dakota." The last was said with derision.

"You sister stood up to your father today," Joanne said, remembering the horror on Dakota's face when she'd realized what kind of man Hector truly was. "I'd have given anything to spare her seeing me like that, but she was there, and she tried to defend me. To stop your father. When it truly mattered, she chose me."

"I guess there's always a first time," Mallory sighed, her anger and bravado evaporating. "I'm just sorry I wasn't there. I should have been." She flushed, and Joanne recognized the signs of guilt.

"Oh, baby, I'm so grateful you weren't there. I'm so thankful that you were safe."

"But he could have killed you all. I heard Dillon talking to Marcus. He had a gun. He...he shot Marcus."

Joanne looked to her son again. "You're all right?"

"Just a graze." Marcus's smile finally reached his eyes. "I'm fine, Mom. As you said, we're all a bit battered but we're going to be okay."

"Yeah," Mallory said. "We've got each other."

"And half of Storm, if the crowd outside in the waiting room is anything to speak of. Hannah and Tucker are out there. And Kristin and Hedda. And Tate Johnson. There's a whole crew."

"And Luis would be here if he could," Mallory said, "only Ginny is in labor, so he's just down the hall."

"Ginny's having the baby?" Joanne smiled, the movement painful but the emotion genuine. "Is everything going okay?"

"Yeah, she's fine. It's just going slowly because it's her first. I think the other half of the town is over there in the OB waiting room. And I saw Logan go into her room." She lifted her eyebrows suggestively.

"Well, they deserve to be happy," Joanne said. "I never thought people should have ostracized Ginny the way that they did. She made a bad choice. It happens to the best of us." An understatement, surely. "But she was smart. She walked away from the senator. That has to count for something."

"I think Logan knows that," Marcus said.

"And Brittany?" Joanne asked. "Does she know about all of this?"

"Yes. She's with her aunt over in the OB lounge. But I told her everything. I didn't want her hearing it from someone else first."

"This isn't going to sit well with her grandmother. I'm so sorry to have made more trouble for the two of you."

"Stop apologizing, Mom," Marcus said, shaking his head. "Dad was the one who caused all of this, not you. He's at fault. He's always been at fault. You got caught up in his madness is all. Hell, if anyone should have done something differently, it's me. I should have forced you to walk away."

"You tried, Marcus. But I truly believed that if I stayed, it would deflect your father's anger from the three of you." She allowed herself a small self-deprecating grin. "Maybe not the soundest of thinking."

"Yeah, well, I say we make a new start," Mallory said. "The three of us." She hesitated for a moment, then shrugged. "And Dakota, if she's willing."

"Whether she's willing or not, she's part of this family, squirt." Marcus gave her a pointed stare.

"Yeah, I suppose so. And I'm not a squirt anymore."

Marcus leaned over to give her a hug. "No, you're not. But in my mind you'll always be my tag-along little sister."

Joanne smiled, watching her children, feeling the smallest stirrings of hope.

"I guess there are worse things," Mallory grumbled.

"Is this a private party?" a deep voice asked from the doorway. "Or can anyone come in?" Dillon Murphy looked decidedly uncomfortable, as if he wasn't quite sure of his welcome.

"Come on in," Marcus said. "The doctor said not to have too many people in here at once. But we were just leaving."

Mallory opened her mouth to protest, but Marcus shot his sister a warning glance. Joanne swallowed a smile.

"We'll be right outside, Mom," Marcus said as he ushered his sister out the door.

Chapter 7

Dillon stood in the doorway, literally hat in hand as Joanne watched her children leave the room. He looked so tall and handsome. So strong and yet so gentle. Everything she wanted in a man. Which after everything that had happened, seemed a mean twist of fate. How could he ever love her? She'd made such a muck of things. Almost destroyed her children's lives.

How could Dillon Murphy ever look at her as anything other than weak and foolish?

"I…ah…wasn't sure you'd want to see me." He looked nervous, his big hands spinning the hat between his fingers.

"Of course I want to see you. You saved my family today."

"It wasn't just me, Joanne. You had a part in saving them too." He walked over to the chair beside the bed. "Can I sit?"

"Please." She gestured to the chair, offering him a shaky smile.

They sat for a moment in silence, the air seeming heavy with all that stretched between them.

"I'm sorry—" they both began at once, then broke off, silence swallowing their words.

"What have you got to be sorry for, Dillon?" she asked, not able to cover the shock in her voice.

"A lot. For lying to you about my part in Hector's leaving. Hell, for getting involved in the first place. I should have talked to you first."

She shook her head, wishing that there was a way to turn back the clock. To change everything. To make it all go away. "You know I wouldn't have listened."

"Maybe not, but there's still what happened today..." He trailed off, looking down at his hat. "I'm not apologizing for what I did. I'd do it over again in a heartbeat. Hector Alvarez was scum. But he was also your husband. And I killed him."

"He wasn't my husband—at least not in any positive sense of that word." She shook her head, needing him to know that there was nothing about today that she regretted. It was the past that held pain. Her decisions, her failures that ate at her core. "A husband is supposed to love and protect. To be a life partner. Hector was none of those things. Not ever. And you—you've been there for me practically every day of my life. You've saved me so many times I've lost count. I'm the one who should be asking for forgiveness. I should have been stronger. I should have been braver. I should have walked out the door."

"You stayed to protect your kids." He reached up to caress her battered face, and she reveled in the contact.

"Yes." She nodded, covering his hand with hers, touching him giving her strength. She needed to say it out loud. To admit to her failings. "But I also stayed because I was scared. And because I didn't think I deserved anything better. If anyone should be sorry, Dillon, it's me. I threw away everything I had all those years ago when I decided to chase after Hector. And everything that's happened since...well, I made my own bed."

"People make mistakes, Joanne. That doesn't mean they have to pay for them forever. And they sure as hell don't deserve to be beaten to death because of them. One thing I can tell you for certain is that what Hector did to you wasn't your fault. That's all on him. And anything you might think to the contrary is just plain wrong."

"In here," she pointed to her head, "I know you're right. I know that I can be a better woman—a stronger woman—than I was when I was with him. But every single day I have to live with what all of this has done to my children. What kind of mother lets her children stay in that kind of situation? I should have found the courage to walk away, Dillon. I should have been stronger for Mallory and Marcus and Dakota."

Her gut clenched, her heart twisting in agony. It felt as if parts of her were being ripped in two. She bent her head, sobs ripping through her, threatening to tear her apart. The physical pain faded against the turmoil and anguish washing through her. She was nothing. No one.

And then his strong arms came around her, his warmth enveloping her.

He held her while she cried. For the things she'd done. For the things she hadn't done. For all that she'd lost. And for all that the world had given her anyway. He whispered nonsensical words of comfort in her ear, and she tried to remember the last time someone had held her just because they cared.

"Let it go," he whispered. "Let it all go. It's time, Joanne. It's over now. It's all over."

Finally the sobs turned to little hiccups, the tears slowing until she could breathe easily again. She pulled back, lifting her gaze to meet his. "I don't know what I would have done if you hadn't come through that door today."

His smile was slow and sure, his big hand rubbing soothing circles against her back. "Well, now, the good news is that you don't have to worry about that. I was there. And I figure I probably always will be. It's just the way things are."

She felt tears again and tried to push them away with her good hand, but he lifted her chin instead, the look in his eyes making her quiver inside. "Because you're the sheriff." She tried for a smile, but knew it was lopsided at best.

"No," he shook his head. "Because I love you." His breath caressed her cheek as he bent to cover her lips with his. The kiss was gentle yet full of promise. And Joanne closed her eyes and let herself feel cherished.

A long while later, he pulled back, staring down at her. "I know you've been through hell, Joanne, but if you'll let me, I want to show you that it doesn't have to be like that."

Hope bloomed, bright and strong, casting light through the dark corners of her soul. "So then maybe there's still a chance for you and me?"

"More than a chance, Joanne." His smile was so wonderful her heart actually lurched in response. "Way, way more than a chance."

* * * *

"What do you mean she turned you down?" Marylee Rush asked her son, fighting against her own irritation.

"Just what I said. I told her I was willing to take care of both her and the child, and she not only said no, she basically told me to go to hell."

"And I take it you didn't respond well to her dismissal." Marylee already knew the answer. She loved her handsome son, but he'd never been able to control his temper or his libido, and they'd both gotten him into trouble more often than not. It's a wonder she'd managed to get him where he was. Now it was a matter of keeping him there. No matter the cost. Even if it meant playing up to the likes of Ginny Moreno.

"I'll admit I lost my temper. Said a few things I shouldn't have said. But the bitch wouldn't even listen." Sebastian threw up his hands in agitation. "To think I was going to offer to marry the little tramp."

"Darling, you can't marry Ginny until you rid yourself of Payton."

"Well, that shouldn't be hard. She's already left me for all practical purposes."

"Yes, and taken up with that Francine Hoffman woman, if the rumors are true." Marylee shuddered delicately. It was hard to fathom Payton taking up with anyone, but if it was Francine, then that explained a lot of things.

"Doesn't matter. Only gives me the higher ground. Infidelity vs. infidelity. And given the predilections, I should win."

"It's a close call." Marylee sighed and wondered again why the hell she hadn't put her considerable influence behind her daughter instead of her son. Sebastian was a man. Which made him a liability in so very many ways. Still, the dice were cast, and she wasn't about to come up with a bad roll.

"What we have to do now," she said, "is figure out how to get control of the baby. It's the best way to be certain this doesn't rise up in the future and bite you in the ass. You made a mistake, you're sorry you did it, and now you want to make it right—with or without Ginny Moreno's cooperation. I already have our lawyers on it. But I think it's equally important that there are witnesses to your change of heart."

Sebastian nodded, adjusting his cufflinks, his expression thoughtful. "You want me to go to the hospital."

"Yes. I think you need to be there for the birth of your son or daughter."

"What about Brittany and Jeffry?"

"What about them?" She frowned, thoughts of her grandchildren as usual filling her with disappointment. Each of them had betrayed the family in their own way. Jeffry by acting out in a very public way and Brittany by taking up with Marcus Alvarez.

"They'll be at the hospital, if for no other reason than to support Celeste. She's still harboring the misguided notion that the baby is actually Jacob's. And anyway, Brittany and Jeffry aren't exactly my biggest fans at the moment."

"You're their father," Marylee snapped. "Handle them. Besides, Brittany will probably be with the Alvarez kid. Hector's death and Joanne's hospitalization will have Marcus running in circles. And Brittany won't stray from his side. If nothing else, my granddaughter is loyal to a fault."

"To everyone but her family."

"Sebastian, do not for a minute think that I don't hold you responsible for this entire mess. If you'd only managed to keep your pants zipped while inside the city limits of Storm, none of this would be happening."

"I slept with Ginny in Austin."

"Yes, but she was Brittany's best friend."

"And a damn good lay. Better than that bitch Dakota."

"Who you did seduce right here in the middle of town.

Outside the Bluebonnet, among other places. What have I ever done to deserve such stupidity?"

"Now, Mother, it's not as if we can't handle this. You said yourself that cream always rises to the top."

"Yes, but it turns out I might not have been talking about you."

For a moment Sebastian looked angry, and then he seemed to collapse. "I'm sorry, Mother. I fucked up. I assumed both of those girls were beneath anyone's notice."

"You know what they say about assuming..." She trailed off and shot him what she hoped was a quelling look. The secret to handling men was to make them believe one never doubted one's self or one's decisions, and that there was always a way to make their lives hell if they didn't follow one's guidance. Marylee had perfected this practice first on Sebastian's father and then on her son.

"Anyway, darling, the important thing now is to show the world that you're going to love your new baby—and if she's amenable, the baby's mother."

"And if she's not?"

Marylee shrugged. "Then we'll destroy her."

* * * *

"It's not going to be long now." The doctor smiled as he pulled off his surgical gloves.

Logan fought the urge to puke. After all the things he'd faced in his life, it surprised the hell out of him that Ginny having a baby would be the event that brought him to his knees. But the idea of her in pain. Well, it was almost too much to bear.

Still, the end result would be worth it. Her baby—their baby—would make his or her entrance into the world. He'd meant what he'd told her. No one and nothing was going to keep them from building a family together. Not the Salts and not the senator.

"I'll be back in a little while to check in," the doctor said. "And if anything happens before that, the nurse will be monitoring." The doctor strode from the room, and Logan returned to the chair by Ginny's bed. Marisol sat across from them, her gaze alternating between concern for her sister and grudging acceptance of his presence.

"Can I get you anything?" Marisol was asking.

Ginny shook her head as she reached for Logan's hand. "I've got everything I need right here."

They'd given her an epidural, which meant the pain wasn't as intense as it had been. A good thing for his hand; he'd thought a couple of times she was going to re-break the finger he'd already broken. The woman had quite a grip on her.

He looked down at her, feeling more helpless than he'd felt in his entire life. Having a baby was supposed to be a natural thing, right? Surely there was nothing to worry about.

"She's doing fine," Marisol reassured him from across the bed. For the first time since he'd arrived, she actually hadn't glared at him. Clearly, his concern was showing.

"I just hate that it has to hurt so much."

"It's better now with the drugs." Ginny squeezed his hand and smiled up at him. His heart almost somersaulted right out of his chest. How had he ever thought he could live without her smiles?

For a moment it was just the two of them, Marisol's presence forgotten as they relished the joy of being together. He'd have a whole lifetime of this if he was lucky. Well, not sitting in a hospital room, but staring into her gorgeous eyes.

"I hate to interrupt," a voice from the door said, and Logan pulled away from Ginny to see Francine Hoffman standing in the doorway. Not much of a surprise really, considering she was a nurse, but something sent a flicker of worry chasing up Logan's spine. Beneath his fingers, he felt Ginny's hand tense.

Automatically he glanced at the monitor tracking her contractions, but she wasn't having one.

"What is it?" he asked, his question coming out more harshly than he'd meant.

"I've got some news." Francine's attention was focused on Ginny as she subtly tipped her head to both Marisol and Logan.

"It's okay, Francine," Ginny said. "Whatever you've come to tell me, I want them here. They're a part of this, too."

"What does she have to tell you?" Logan frowned, fighting his rising concern.

Ginny swallowed, pulling her hand free. "A while ago, after the first time the senator threatened me, I asked Francine to do a paternity test. I figured it was better to know what I was facing. To be prepared for whatever came next."

Logan fought a wave of both pride and guilt. Pride because Ginny was so fierce and amazing when it came to taking care of her child. And guilt because he should have been facing these demons with her and instead he'd been wallowing in his own self-serving hell.

"All right, then," Francine said, her voice matter-of-fact as she slit open the sealed envelope she held.

"Wait." Logan held up a hand. Francine and Marisol both looked surprised. Ginny looked worried. He smiled down at her. "I just wanted to say that whatever we find out, I meant what I said earlier. It doesn't matter. As far as I'm concerned, this baby is mine. And I'm going to honor both of you for the rest of my life."

Tears filled Ginny's eyes as he reached over to run his fingers across her cheek.

Across the bed, Marisol was beaming at him. And Francine cleared her throat, her eyes looking suspiciously moist. "So," she said, pulling out a sheet of paper. "Do you want me to do the honors?"

Ginny nodded, slipping her hand into Logan's.

Francine pulled opened the report just as Senator Rush burst through the door.

"What the hell is he doing here?" the senator asked, his eyes narrowing on Logan.

"He's here because he's family," Marisol said, rising to her feet even as Logan jumped to his.

"If anyone should be here with Ginny, it should be me," the senator snarled, his face mottled with anger. "I'm the baby's father."

"Actually," Francine said, looking up from the report, her face wreathed in a smile. "You're not." She held the report out to Logan, who was already halfway across the room, his mind focused on kicking the senator's ass. At her words, he froze.

"He's not?" Hand shaking, he took the report and scanned it quickly, his smile followed by a war whoop. "Holy shit, Ginny, the baby is Jacob's. Little Bit is Jacob's."

The senator tried to snatch the piece of paper away, but Logan was faster, his joy turning to anger as he flanked the older man. "In deference to the ladies, I'm going to give you one warning." His voice grew lower as he closed the distance between him and the senator. "You have no business here. Your involvement with my family is over. Do you understand what I'm saying?"

The senator held his ground, his expression masked. "The baby is mine," he asserted, but there was doubt in his voice now.

"Not according to this report," Logan said. "And now unless you'd like me to call security, I want you to leave. And if I ever catch you anywhere near Ginny or the baby, I promise you'll live to regret it. Am I making myself clear?"

"Perfectly," the senator replied, his chin rising as he straightened both of his cuffs. "I'll leave you and your little whore to your bastard baby."

Logan didn't even pause to think, he just swung, catching the belligerent bastard right in the face. There was a satisfying crunch as the senator stumbled backward, blood spurting from his nose.

Security arrived at that moment, saving the senator from the rest of Logan's anger. As they hauled the senator out of the room, Logan turned back to face the ladies, not completely certain of his reception.

"That was amazing," Marisol said.

"Awesome," Francine echoed.

"Wonderful." Ginny smiled, and then grimaced. "But I think maybe now we need to concentrate on having the baby."

"Jacob's baby," Logan said, moving quickly to her side.

"No," she whispered, her gaze locking on his. "Ours."

Chapter 8

"How's your mom?" Brittany asked as Marcus sat down beside her in the waiting room.

The place was almost standing room only. Celeste and Payton huddled in one corner with Ian and Jeffry. Mallory, Luis, and Lacey were standing by the coffee machine. Sonya and Aiden Murphy were there as well, along with Logan's grandfather Michael. It was practically a town meeting. Or maybe just a large extended family.

"She's going to be okay," Marcus answered. "Dillon is with her now. I think maybe finally, they're going to get a chance to figure out what's going on between the two of them."

"Your mother deserves a chance at happiness after everything your dad put her through."

"You're right. It's just kind of hard to wrap my head around Dillon and my mom. You know? I mean, hell, he's the sheriff. Not exactly the kind of dude I'd have wanted to be my stepfather back in the day."

"Well, you've changed," she said, punching him playfully on his uninjured arm. "You're a model citizen these days."

He leaned over to steal a kiss. "Don't count on it, sweetheart. There's still a lot of wickedness left in this boy."

She grinned, then her expression grew serious. "Mallory seems to be dealing okay."

His gaze moved to his youngest sister as she laughed at

something Luis was saying. "She's coping at least. I think it helps to be young. And she's always kept her distance from Hector. So I suspect she's better equipped to deal with his death than Mom or Dakota."

"What about Dakota?" Brittany asked. "Do you know where she is?"

He sucked in a painful breath. "She was at the lake. Patrick found her. He said she's pretty shaken up. He's bringing her here."

"This is going to be especially hard on her. She worshiped Hector. It's tough having the rug pulled out from under you."

"I'll admit part of me thinks she deserves it. But mostly I think she's just a really damaged kid. You know?"

"I do. And I know that she's not the only one hurting." Brittany's hand found his, and he reveled in the comfort just her touch brought. "I can't imagine what you must be feeling."

"To be honest, I'm not sure I even know what I'm feeling. I mean, I hate what my father has done to my family. And I know that some part of me ought to be sorry that he's dead. But I'm not. I'm just not."

"I understand what it is to have a despicable father, believe me. Mine was just here, as a matter of fact."

"Ah, shit. Did he go in to see Ginny?"

"He did. Forced his way in, actually, and came out sporting a bloody nose that I think probably is going to ruin his profile in the next election."

"Logan?" Marcus asked, not able to squelch his satisfied smile.

"Yeah. He's in there with Ginny."

He sobered, turning to face the woman he loved. "I'm sorry. I didn't mean to take pleasure in your dad's pain."

"Why?" Brittany asked, her lips curling into a soft smile. "I did. He made his bed and all that… I'm just glad that Ginny and Dakota got away from him. I don't even blame Dakota for outing him anymore. He deserved that, too."

"Yeah, but not the rest of the people she hurt in the process."

"Maybe not. But with any luck, we can all move forward from here and get on with our lives."

"Do you mean that?"

"Of course I do." She shook her head, her expression confused and adorable.

"Good," he said, brushing a strand of hair back from her face. "Because I have news."

"More? I mean it's been a rather eventful day between Ginny's going into labor and your father's...well... you know."

"Death? It's okay. You can say it. Bastard deserved it."

"That doesn't mean it doesn't hurt."

"His betrayal is what hurt. The fact that he's gone can only be a good thing. For all of us. Anyway, my news isn't quite as mind-altering as all that, but Ian finalized the deal on some land. The ranch is going to be a reality. Ian's staying in town."

Brittany shot a look at his mentor. "Marisol."

"Yeah, pretty much." Marcus nodded at his friend, happy that he'd found someone to share his life with.

"But what does that mean for you?" Brittany's brows drew together in a frown. "I mean if Ian is staying here?"

"He's going to oversee both of his operations from here. The one in Montana and the one here. But I'm going to be running the place here. Ian asked me to be his partner."

"Oh my God, Marcus, that's wonderful. You'll do an amazing job. I know you'll make Ian proud."

"Well, I'm kind of hoping that you'll be the one who's proud. And that you'll consider sticking around and being a part of my success. I know you have to finish college. But maybe you can stick with the online courses? Or maybe commute to somewhere closer than Austin?"

"What are you saying, Marcus?"

"I'm saying that I want you with me. Always. But I don't want you to substitute your dreams for mine."

Her smile could have lit all of Storm. "My dreams are your dreams, Marcus. Together we can do anything."

Voices rose with excitement as Francine walked into the waiting room.

"So," she said, her smile embracing them all, "I'm happy to say that Storm's newest resident has made a squalling healthy entrance. I know you'll all join me in welcoming Jacob Logan Moreno. Mother and baby are doing fine."

Marcus watched as Brittany's aunt reached for her mother's hand, tears streaming down her face. "Jacob?" Celeste whispered, the hope in her eyes making Marcus's heart stutter.

Francine nodded. "Just like his papa."

* * * *

"You ready for this?" Patrick asked as he and Dakota stepped off of the hospital elevator.

She blew out a long breath. "I don't know. I'm not sure what I'm supposed to say. I mean after everything I've done."

"You'll be fine. Your mother loves you. And for that matter, so do your brother and sister." He nodded to where Mallory and Marcus were standing waiting for her.

"I don't know about that." She reached for Patrick's hand, surprising herself as much as him.

"No." He shook his head, his blue eyes full of compassion she probably didn't deserve. But she liked the way it felt anyway. "This is something you have to do for yourself. I'll be here when you're done."

For a moment she wavered, and then she nodded, turning to close the distance between her and her siblings. "Hi," she said, feeling like an idiot, but not knowing what else to say. "How's your arm?"

"It's just a graze," Marcus said with a shrug. "How are you?"

"I've been better." She tried for a smile and failed miserably. "But at least I didn't get shot."

"Oh, Dakota, I can't even imagine what it must have been like," Mallory said, her baby sister reaching out to grab her hands. "I'm just glad you're okay. Where have you been?"

"I, ah… I've been at the lake. Thinking."

Marcus nodded. "I figured you'd go there."

"Did you send Patrick?" She frowned, suddenly wondering if Patrick's concern was Marcus's doing.

"No. He volunteered. I just steered him in the right direction."

"How's Mom?"

"She's beat up. And it's going to take a while for the injuries to heal. But she's going to be okay."

Dakota wished like hell that healing would truly be as simple as a few mended bones.

"She's been asking for you," Mallory said.

"Oh, God." Tears threatened and Dakota stared at the ceiling, trying to get her tumbling emotions under control. "I'm not sure I know why."

"Because she's worried about you. I mean you were there when...when..."

"It's okay, Mal," Marcus said. "You can say it. Dad is dead."

Dakota felt a fresh stab of pain. "Is he...I mean is the body..."

"The sheriff's department took him to the morgue."

She nodded, her stomach clenching as the memory of the day's horror played again through her mind. "And Sheriff Murphy? He's not...he's not in trouble, right? I mean, he was defending us."

Marcus looked surprised, and she felt ashamed that he'd doubt her stance on how things played out. "He's going to be fine. There were plenty of witnesses."

"I'll be happy to give a statement if it helps," she said, wishing there was something more she could do. Like wipe out the last five or six years of her life.

"I'll let Dillon know." He paused for a minute, his gaze searching hers. "Do you want to see Mom?"

Yes. No. God, if only it were as simple as one or the other. She pulled in a ragged breath. "Yeah. I do."

"Good for you," Mallory said, her smile giving Dakota a moment of peace. Of all of them, their father's malevolence had touched her the least. Which was something good to hold onto. "Do you want us to come with you?"

Her eyes met Marcus's again. "No. Patrick's right. This is something I have to do myself."

For a moment she thought she saw a flash of pride in Marcus's eyes, but of course after everything she'd done, that wasn't possible. Still, just the idea made her feel stronger. "Dakota, you know that none of what happened at the house was your fault."

"Maybe not directly. But we are where we are in part because of my actions. And pretending otherwise isn't going to change the facts."

This time she was certain it was a sparkle of pride. Too little too late, but she'd cherish it anyway.

"Ready?" Marcus asked as they came to a closed hospital room door.

"As I'll ever be." She reached for the door handle, and then stopped for a moment to look back at her brother. "Marcus?"

"Yeah?" he replied, his eyebrows raised in question.

"I'm sorry. For everything."

"I know. Honest to God, I do. And believe me, I sure as hell know what it feels like to spiral out of control."

She held his gaze for a minute, and then pushed open the door and walked into her mother's room.

Joanne was lying back against her pillows, her face turning every conceivable shade of purple and blue. Her arm was in a splint and monitors beeped incessantly behind her as various machines kept track of her vital statistics. She looked so small and helpless. And yet in Dakota's mind's eye, all she could see was her mother leaping in front of her, drawing her father's wrath away from her. The truth was that Dakota's mother was the opposite of small and helpless.

She'd stood strong against a monster for years. She'd taken beatings just so that Dakota and Marcus and Mallory would be safe. Everything good in Dakota's life was due to her mother's diligence. And she'd thrown it all back in her mother's face at every opportunity. Shame washed through her, hot and heavy, threatening to tear her into pieces.

"Oh, honey," Joanne said, holding out her arms. "Come

here. Let me see you. I just want to know you're okay."

Dakota felt the tears fall as she ran to her mother's side. "Oh, God, Mom, I thought he was going to kill you."

Joanne smiled through her own tears. "I thought he was going to kill you."

"But he didn't. We're here. And we're alive. And he…" She swallowed, trying so hard to make sense of this new reality. "He's dead."

"I'm so sorry, baby. I know you loved him." Joanne reached out to stroke her hair, the gesture bringing memories of so many other times when she'd done just the same.

"No." She shook her head. "I loved the idea of him. But the father I believed in never existed. I was lying to myself, Momma, and because of that I hurt you so much. I'm the one who's sorry. How can you ever forgive me?"

"There's nothing to forgive. You're my child, Dakota. From the first moment they laid you in my arms, I loved you. And there's nothing you can ever do that will change that fact. Nothing."

Dakota gave her mother a watery smile. "Well, you've got to admit I gave it a good try."

"You were always my wild child. And you know what's really funny about that? I was just like you when I was growing up. I hated this town. And I hated the restrictions my family kept trying to put on my life. So I rebelled."

"And married Daddy."

"Yes. But it didn't turn out quite like I'd planned." A shadow passed across her mother's face.

"I'm so sorry. I thought you were making it all up. That you were persecuting Daddy. But all that time, he was… he was…"

"Your father was a very sick man. He wasn't happy with his lot in life, and he chose to take that out on the people around him. I just happened to be the closest person in line."

"And you kept it from us so that we wouldn't get hurt, too."

Joanne's smile was tender. "Like I said, you're my children. Nothing is more precious. I'd happily give my life for any of you."

"You almost did." Dakota wiped away her tears, forcing herself to stand strong. If her mother could do it, so could she. "But at least now it's over. Have you…have you talked to Sheriff Murphy?"

"I have." This time her mother's smile was wistful and hopeful all at the same time. She looked ten years younger.

"And did he propose? I mean, it's pretty obvious he's always been crazy about you."

"No. And even if he did, I wouldn't agree to marry him. At least not now. It's important sometimes to make your own way, Dakota. And as much as I care about Dillon, I need to find myself, figure out who I want to be."

Dakota frowned, confused. "So you're not going to see him?"

"I am. I'm just not going to jump too fast into anything. Right now, I want to concentrate on you and your brother and sister. And I want to help Tate win that election. Truth is, I just need time to heal."

Dakota nodded, although she wasn't sure she completely understood. Wasn't having the right man in your life the goal women were supposed to strive for? At least it had always seemed that way to her.

But then she'd been wrong about most things so far, so maybe this was something else she'd managed to totally screw up. Maybe her mom was right. Maybe the more important thing was to figure out who she truly was—or more importantly, who she wanted to be. Maybe the only one who could really save her was herself.

Crazy notion.

But then again, maybe not.

* * * *

Celeste stood outside Ginny's room wanting so much to walk through the door and at the same time being terrified to do so. Her grandson was waiting inside. Jacob's son. Jacob's, Ginny's—

and Logan's. As much as she'd struggled with the idea, she knew now that the two of them belonged together. And that what they felt for each other had nothing to do with how Ginny had felt about Jacob. Or how Ginny felt about his son.

Lost in her own grief, Celeste had almost lost the most important gift Jacob could have left behind. A piece of himself. Made in a moment of love with his very best friend—of that she was convinced.

She also knew in her heart, that this new life, this new Jacob, could never replace her son. And that the idea she'd even entertained the thought for a second was ludicrous. But now, if Ginny could forgive her, she had a chance to be a part of this new family.

Everything around her was shifting and changing. Her sister's life. Her niece's and nephew's. Even Travis had a new direction, though she'd heard through the grapevine it wouldn't be with Kristin. The point was that this was her chance for something new. For something better. With her daughters. With her sister and her family. And with her new grandchild.

Sucking in a fortifying breath, Celeste pasted on a smile and walked into the room. Ginny lay propped up against the pillows, Logan sitting on the bed beside her, the baby wrapped in a blue blanket cuddled in Ginny's arms.

It was a miracle in the truest sense of the word. And Celeste prayed that they'd let her be a part of it.

"I hope it's okay that I came," she said.

"Of course it is," Ginny replied with a beaming smile. Logan slid a possessive arm around her shoulders, his look not nearly as welcoming. Not that Celeste blamed him. "I know you're dying to meet your grandson," Ginny continued.

Celeste wasn't sure she'd ever heard sweeter words, but she held her ground. "I am, but first I need to apologize to you. I didn't handle any of this very well. And I wasn't kind to you. I didn't even try to understand."

"I was the one who lied," Ginny said. "You had every right to be upset. And as far as I'm concerned, it's all water under the bridge."

"Well, for what it's worth, I'm truly sorry. And if you'll let me," she paused, her gaze moving to Logan, "if *both* of you will let me, I'd like to be a part of the baby's life. Only as much as you'll allow, of course." She searched their faces, looking for some sign that they weren't going to throw her out of the room. "I don't want you to think I'm going to try and take over or demand more than is warranted under the circumstances. I realize I haven't given you any reason to believe that, but..."

"Celeste," Logan said, raising a hand to stop her. "We want you to be a part of Jake's life."

"Jake." She repeated the word like a prayer.

"Yeah," Ginny said, stroking her son's silky cheek. "It's too hard to call him Jacob. You know?"

Celeste nodded, still rooted to the spot.

"He's got Jacob's eyes," Ginny said, this time shifting to offer the little boy, who was squirming, tiny fists flying as he scrunched up his face.

Celeste walked over to the bed, sitting down in the chair beside it, her heart pounding as she held out a hand and Jake grabbed a finger. "It's too early to know for sure," she said. "Their eyes can change color still."

"I know, but look at him," Ginny said. "He's got Jacob's smile, too. And that isn't going to change."

Ginny held out the baby, and Celeste tenderly took him into her arms. He was so precious. So beautiful.

"I think he looks like Ginny, too," Logan said, his arm still around her, but he was smiling now, looking down at the baby, his eyes full of love.

"Definitely. Especially all that curly dark hair." Celeste smiled. "You're both going to be amazing parents." And in that moment, Celeste realized she truly meant that. Had Jacob lived, things would surely have been very different, but it seemed somehow that things had worked out okay anyway. Life always found a way. She of all people should know that.

Ginny blushed and Logan's arm tightened around her. "We are going to be good parents," he agreed. "And what we don't work out on our own, you and Marisol and my mother will make sure we figure out."

"It takes a village," Celeste said with her first true smile. "Or, whether you like it or not, at least half the people in Storm."

"I heard about Travis," Ginny said, her face full of concern. "I'm so sorry."

"Don't be." Celeste shook her head, rocking her beautiful grandson. "It was a long time coming. And we're all going to be better because of it. I truly believe that. What we have to do now is concentrate on the future." She cooed at the baby, then looked up at Ginny and Logan with a smile. "And from where I'm sitting, it's looking pretty bright."

Chapter 9

Lacey sucked in a breath and looked out across the crowd gathered for the dedication of Jacob's bench as Pastor Douglas recited a prayer. Her mother and her aunt stood off to one side with Francine Hoffman. Lacey had to admit that despite everything, Celeste looked really good. For the first time in forever, she seemed to be more herself.

Her father stood at the opposite side of the gathering, looking tall and handsome and maybe a little lost. She and Sara Jane had been spending time with him at their mother's urging. Funny that, even though she'd all but washed her hands of him, her mother was still watching out for her dad. Lacey smiled, thinking that Jacob would have been proud of Celeste.

Once he'd gotten over the enormity of being a father.

Close to where her mom and aunt were standing, Ginny and Logan stood surrounded by various Murphys and Morenos, including Mallory and Luis, who grinned and waved when they caught her eye. Ginny was holding baby Jake. Jacob's son. Her nephew. Lacey's stomach clenched at the enormity of it all.

It had been almost a month since her life and half the town's had literally imploded around them. Hector Alvarez was dead, which to hear most tell was a blessing. But Lacey knew that he'd left behind a legacy that wouldn't easily be forgotten. Mallory's mom was getting better. Stronger every day. She'd resumed working Tate's campaign, and she and the sheriff had been seen out and about more than once.

Marcus and Brit seemed to be settling down. He'd even started building a ranch house out on some land he and Ian Briggs owned. And Ginny and Logan had made it official. They were getting married. Which seemed like a good thing. Something her brother would probably approve of.

The senator and his mother had left town. Simply pulled up stakes and moved to Austin. Well, they still had the house here, but thankfully, they'd moved on to greener pastures. At least for now. It made life easier for Jeffry, who was talking to Scott and Max. He waved when she caught his eye, looking more happy and relaxed than he had in years.

Chase and Anna Mae were holding hands while Rita Mae was deep in conversation with Tate, Mary Louise Prager, and Tate's dad, while Tate's brother Tucker was totally absorbed in Hannah Grossman.

Seemed like there was a rash of domestic bliss in the air. Lacey felt a little twinge of envy, and then shook her head. She was way too young to worry about settling down. As if to underscore the point, or maybe just the opposite, Max Marshall chose that moment to send her a wolfish grin. Maybe there was something to all this boy-needs-girl stuff after all. Her lips curled up in an answering smile.

"You ready?" Sara Jane said, interrupting her flirtation with Max, the pastor just finishing the invocation.

"Yeah," Lacey said, smiling at her sister. It was time. Time to honor her brother. Time to recognize all that he was. Time to let him finally rest in peace. She moved to the podium and looked out across the gathered group of people. Friends, acquaintances, and family. She'd lived here her whole life. And seeing everyone come together to honor her brother, she realized just how lucky she'd been to grow up in a place like Storm.

"Thank y'all for coming. I'd like to think that Jacob can see all of you and know how very much he was loved. He wasn't here with us for nearly as long as we would have wanted or he deserved, but the time he was with us..." Her gaze moved to

Ginny. "Well, he made it count. He was a loyal friend. And a wonderful son. And the best brother ever. And if he could have been here now, I know he'd have made an amazing father."

She swallowed, tears pricking the back of her eyes. "But I also know that even though he's gone, he lives on in each of us. He will always be a part of the fabric of Storm. He'll live on in our memories. And we'll see him in Jake's smile. And when we sit here on this bench, we'll think of him. Of all that he was. And all that he gave us."

Lacey smiled through her tears, her gaze moving from her sister to her father and finally to her mother. "And so I give you my brother Jacob's bench. And I ask you to remember him always."

Everyone clapped and smiled, and Lacey stepped away from the podium, her mother waiting for her off to the side.

"I'm so proud of you, sweetheart. And Jacob would be proud, too." Her mother had come so far from the day she'd found her in the cemetery. "It was a lovely thing to do."

"I just wanted everyone to be able to remember him." She hugged her mother and then turned to the other people waiting to commend her on the presentation of the bench.

Finally, everyone made their way to the parish hall where Tara and the other ladies of the church had laid out a fabulous spread.

Ginny stopped Lacey as she walked into the vestibule. "It was really nice what you did today. Jacob would have loved it."

"Well," Lacey grinned, "maybe on the inside, but you know on the outside he'd have been embarrassed by all the attention."

"True." Since the birth of the baby, the two of them had made their peace. Lacey was still ashamed of the way she'd treated Ginny, but the older girl seemed to have totally forgiven her, going so far as to ask her to be Jake's godmother. It was a huge responsibility and it made Lacey proud to think that Ginny trusted her with the job.

Patrick, Logan's brother, was standing in as the godfather.

"Where's Jake?" she asked, pulling her thoughts to the present. The baby was never very far from Ginny's side.

"With your mom and my sister." She nodded to where the two women stood cooing over the baby. "He's just over three weeks old and they're already spoiling him rotten."

"It makes her really happy," Lacey said, watching her mom's look of unadulterated delight. "Thank you for letting her be a part of his life."

"Of course," Ginny was quick to assure.

"I don't know. Considering the way we both treated you after the truth came out, I wouldn't have blamed you for not letting anyone from our family within fifty yards of Jake."

"We all made mistakes, Lacey. Me most of all. And Jacob would want you guys to be a part of Jake's life. And honestly, I do, too." She paused for a moment, and then continued. "How are things with your dad?"

"Different. And difficult. And better, too, if that makes any sense."

"Did you know about him and Kristin?"

"No. I didn't. And now it doesn't really matter. It's time for him to find his own way, you know?"

"Yeah, I do. Anyway, I'm glad your mom's better. And I'm glad we're friends again."

"Me, too."

Ginny gave her a quick hug and moved over to Celeste and Marisol, clearly ready to retrieve her son.

"Hey, you ready to jet?" Jeffry asked. "I know it's kind of your party, but we were all thinking of heading to the lake."

She glanced over to where Mallory, Luis, Scott, and Max were waiting.

From across the room, her mom nodded, telegraphing her approval with the gesture. Lacey returned her mom's nod as she linked arms with Mallory. Life in Storm might be different now, and in all honesty her family would never truly be the same, but Lacey finally had her priorities straight. And thankfully, she had her friends back. And somehow, in the moment, that's the only thing that truly mattered.

That and knowing that wherever he was, Jacob was smiling in approval.

* * * *

"Penny for your thoughts?"

Dakota looked up from her seat on Jacob's bench to see Patrick standing over her. Most everyone had either headed for home or was still inside the parish hall. She'd made an appearance at the dedication, feeling like she owed Jacob that much, but she could only stand the whispers and sideways glances so long.

"I was thinking about Jacob. And Storm." She shrugged. "About my family. All of it, I guess."

"I'm glad you came. It was good that you were here."

"I suspect you're a party of one then. Most everyone in there wishes I'd stayed home. I'm not sure they're ever really going to forgive me for what happened on Founders' Day."

"I think you'll be surprised. It just takes time." He sat down next to her on the bench, his large frame filling the space, the heat of his body comfortable against her side. Patrick Murphy was a good man and she was lucky to be able to call him a friend.

"Maybe so. I suppose we'll see."

He took her hand in his. "It'll all come right, eventually. I promise."

For a moment they just sat there in silence, the soft shadows of the evening falling around them. Fall had finally come to Storm, the temperature dropping as the light faded. Dakota shivered, and Patrick slipped his arm around her.

It would be so easy to lean back into his arms. To let him make her world okay. But if she'd learned anything from her mother, it was the importance of standing on her own two feet. Of believing in herself and not counting on someone else to fix all her troubles for her.

"I want to thank you for standing by me," she said, needing to at least let him know how much he mattered. "I don't think anyone outside of my family has ever done that before." She frowned into the shadows. "I think given the chance, you could become really important to me." She shot him a shy smile, her heart stuttering at the look in his eyes.

"I think you already are important to me."

God, she wanted to give in. To stay here with him forever. But if she did, well, she'd never know what life held in store for her. And now more than ever, with everything that had happened, she needed to find out. It was important. Her mom was right.

She blew out a slow breath, wondering if she was about to make the biggest mistake of her life. "I've decided to leave Storm."

Patrick frowned, his expression confused. "I don't understand."

"I told you about Amanda and College Station when we were at the lake."

"That she'd asked you to come visit. So you're going to take her up on the offer?"

"Well, actually a little more than that. I'm going to stay with her. At least until I get my feet on the ground and get settled."

"I'm not following." If the situation weren't so serious, she'd have laughed at the confusion playing across his face.

"Last week I ran into Milton Waters." Mr. Waters ran the Storm newspaper. "Did you know he owns the Bryan-College Station paper too?" She paused, grateful that he still had his arm around her. "Well, anyway, I told him about going to see Amanda. And about the trouble I've had finding a job here in Storm. So he offered me a job at the paper there. In sales. It's just an entry-level position, but it's a start. And right now, I think I need a new beginning."

"I think it's fantastic," Patrick said, leaning over to kiss her cheek. "You'll be good in sales."

She swallowed a bubble of laughter. "Yeah, pushy broad that I am."

"No. I mean it. I think you'll be great. And I understand why you need to go away. To start over somewhere else."

"It's not like College Station is on another planet," she offered, not really wanting to end things before they'd even begun.

"True enough. And it is my alma mater. I've been known to attend a game or two or three." He smiled, pushing the hair back from her face. "I'm really proud of you, you know. You could have used your father's death as an excuse to spiral out of control. But you didn't. Instead you're trying to take responsibility for your life. That's not an easy thing to do."

"No. It isn't. But it's easier when I can see that my family is going to be okay. Mom has your brother. And Marcus has his new ranch and Brittany. And Mallory has Luis and Lacey."

"When are you leaving?" he asked.

"Later tonight. I stayed until the dedication. But I figure if I don't go now, I might not go at all…" Her throat tightened and her heart started to pound.

He pulled her to her feet, this time his lips finding hers. For a moment, she just let herself enjoy the kiss. Let herself soar away on the rush of emotion. But then she pulled back, needing to distance herself—for once to keep her feet firmly planted on the ground.

"I'm going to miss you," she whispered.

"I'll miss you, too." His smile was tender. "But like you said, it's not like you're going to the moon."

"Exactly."

From across the parking lot, Patrick's parents called his name.

"Go on," she said, giving him a little push before she sat back down on the bench.

For a moment he stood there looking at her, and then with a quick smile he turned to walk away, and Dakota sighed. Tomorrow would mark a new beginning, and somehow that fresh start would mean more because she might actually be leaving something behind.

* * * *

The evening was winding down. Only closest family were left. Celeste, Payton, and Francine stood talking in one corner.

Marisol and Ian were deep in discussion with Marcus and Logan. Logan had Jake parked on his shoulder, the baby looking so tiny and thankfully, sound asleep.

Ginny couldn't resist a smile. It had only been a few weeks since her disastrous encounter with the senator. But her world had done a complete one-eighty since then, everything turning out like some kind of fairytale. She still wasn't sure she deserved the happy ending she'd gotten, but she wasn't foolish enough to turn it down.

One night with Jacob had changed everything. Not in the way she'd expected, surely. But definitely in a way that was infinitely good. Her heart flooded with love as she thought about her best friend. He'd left her with the most beautiful of gifts.

His son.

Fighting tears, she walked from the parish hall out into the chill of the evening. Live oaks arched over her head, streetlamps flickering against their dark leaves. She walked toward Jacob's bench, needing for a moment to be closer to him. But as she moved through the gathering gloom, she realized the bench was already occupied. The fading light gleamed against the bent blonde head, her face buried in her hands.

Dakota.

Ginny almost turned and walked away. And then she thought about all that she'd been given. All that she'd been *for*given, and she knew she couldn't leave without at least acknowledging the other woman.

"I see we had the same idea."

Dakota jerked up, her face wet with tears. "I'm sorry, I'll go."

"No." Ginny shook her head, lifting a hand. "I think it's fitting somehow that the two of us are here together at Jacob's bench."

She sat down beside Dakota, staring up at the shivering trees. "He'd have liked this bench."

"I remember how much he liked the square," Dakota said, her voice quiet—pensive. "I haven't had the chance to talk to you. But I want you to know that I wasn't trying to blow up your life." She paused, sucked in a breath. "Well, maybe I was. I was always so jealous of what you had with Jacob. And then what you have with Logan. So when I found out that you'd been with Sebastian, too. And when he…well, you know what he's capable of. Suffice it to say I didn't take his rejection very well. I was so hurt and angry that I just lashed out the only way I could. And hurt you in the process."

"I made my bed, Dakota." Ginny looked at her and smiled. "Literally. So my pain might have been at your instigation, but it was my own fault, pure and simple."

"But it's all okay, now, right?"

She looked so needy that Ginny didn't have the heart to do anything but reassure her. "It is." She reached over to squeeze Dakota's hand. "And what about you? Are you all right? I mean, so much has happened."

For a moment she thought that Dakota wasn't going to answer. And then she shrugged. "To be honest, most of it really sucks. I mean my father turns out to be a bigger bastard than people always tried to tell me he was. I realized that my actions might actually have made my mother's life worse. And that everything I thought was true about myself was basically bullshit."

"But you're getting a second chance. Just like me."

"Maybe. We'll see. I'm leaving tonight actually. I've got a new job—in College Station."

"Wow." Ginny was surprised to find that she was disappointed that Dakota was leaving. It was almost as if a part of her were going. Their lives had become so intertwined. "But it's a good thing, right?"

"I hope so. It seems like the right decision. I mean, all I've ever wanted to do is get away from here. This is my chance. Except that now that I'm actually going, I'm scared." She turned to meet Ginny's gaze. "That's stupid, right?"

"Not at all." Ginny shook her head. "Life is scary. But that's the beauty of being from a place like Storm. You don't have to be frightened, because no matter what happens to you out there—good or bad—you can always come home. And we'll all be here. Waiting."

For a moment their gazes held, and then Dakota reached over to give Ginny a hug.

"Thank you," she said as she pushed off the bench. "For what it's worth, I'm really glad I know you."

"Me too." Ginny leaned back, feeling Jacob's plaque against her back. "Good luck. And Dakota?" The other girl stopped, looking back over her shoulder. "Be happy."

She nodded as she walked into the twilight.

Ginny lifted her head to the trees, closing her eyes, imagining for just a moment that Jacob was sitting beside her. Not as a boyfriend or husband, but as her best friend. More than anyone else, he'd be glad she'd found her way.

"Hey, you," Logan said, bringing Ginny out of her reverie. "I wondered where you got off to."

"Just wanted a moment of quiet."

Logan sat next to her on the bench. "It's nice to have a little part of him here in the square."

"Yeah," she said, snuggling up next to him. "It is. So where's Jake?"

"With your sister and my mother."

"Like I said, he's going to be one spoiled kid."

"There are worse things that could happen." He tightened his arms around her. "You okay?"

"Better than okay." She smiled up at him. "I've got you and Jake. And a wonderful family. I can't imagine needing anything more."

He kissed the top of her head. "Is that Dakota?" He nodded at the moving figure on the edge of the square.

"Yeah. She was here at the bench. Saying good-bye, I think."

"Good-bye?"

"She's leaving town. Got a new job in College Station." Ginny sighed and Logan pulled her closer.

"Well, I hope she finds what she's looking for."

"Me, too," Ginny said, loving how warm and safe he made her feel.

"You think she's going to be okay?" His breath caressed her ear.

Ginny settled back into his arms, lifting her face for his kiss. "I think she's going to be just fine."

About Dee Davis

Bestselling author Dee Davis has a masters degree in public administration. Prior to writing, she served as the director of two associations, wrote award winning PSAs, did television and radio commercials, starred in the Seven Year Itch, taught college classes, and lobbied both the Texas Legislature and the US Congress.

Her highly acclaimed first novel, Everything In Its Time, was published in July 2000. Since then, among others, she's won the Booksellers Best, Golden Leaf, Texas Gold and Prism awards, and been nominated for the National Readers Choice Award, the Holt and two RT Reviewers Choice Awards.

Recently she was honored with a Lifetime Achievement Award from the New York Romance Writers and has also been nominated for a Lifetime Achievement Award for romantic suspense from Romantic Times. In addition, she is a Hall of Fame member of the New Jersey Romance Writers and was awarded an Odyssey Medal from Hendrix College.

To date, she has written over thirty romantic suspense, time travel, and women's fiction novels and novellas. Among her latest books you'll find her A-Tac, Liar's Game, and Last Chance series.

She's lived in Austria and traveled in Europe extensively. And although she now resides in an 1802 farmhouse in Connecticut, she still calls Texas home.

Connect with Dee online:
Website: http://www.deedavis.com
Facebook: http://www.facebook.com/deedavisbooks
Twitter: http://twitter.com/deesdavis @deeSdavis

Sign up for the Rising Storm/1001 Dark Nights Newsletter
and be entered to win an exclusive lightning bolt necklace
specially designed for Rising Storm by
Janet Cadsawan of Cadsawan.com.

Go to www.RisingStormBooks.com to subscribe.

As a bonus, all subscribers will receive a free
Rising Storm story
Storm Season: Ginny & Jacob – the Prequel
by Dee Davis

Rising Storm

Storm, Texas.

Where passion runs hot, desire runs deep, and secrets have the power to destroy...

Nestled among rolling hills and painted with vibrant wildflowers, the bucolic town of Storm, Texas, seems like nothing short of perfection.

But there are secrets beneath the facade. Dark secrets. Powerful secrets. The kind that can destroy lives and tear families apart. The kind that can cut through a town like a tempest, leaving jealousy and destruction in its wake, along with shattered hopes and broken dreams. All it takes is one little thing to shatter that polish.

Rising Storm is a series conceived by Julie Kenner and Dee Davis to read like an on-going drama. Set in a small Texas town, *Rising Storm* is full of scandal, deceit, romance, passion, and secrets. Lots of secrets.

Look for other Rising Storm Season 2 titles, now available! (And if you missed Season 1 and the midseason episodes, you can find those titles here!)

Rising Storm, Season Two

Against the Wind by Rebecca Zanetti

As Tate Johnson works to find a balance between his ambitions for political office and the fallout of his brother's betrayal, Zeke is confronted with his brother Chase's return home. And while Bryce and Tara Daniels try to hold onto their marriage, Kristin continues to entice Travis into breaking his vows...

Storm Warning by Larissa Ione
As Joanne Alvarez settles into life without Hector, her children still struggle with the fallout. Marcus confronts the differences between him and Brittany, while Dakota tries to find a new equilibrium. Meanwhile, the Johnson's grapple with war between two sets of brothers, and Ian Briggs rides into town...

Brave the Storm by Lisa Mondello
As Senator Rush's poll numbers free fall, Marylee tries to drive a wedge between Brittany and Marcus. Across town, Anna Mae and Chase dance toward reconciliation. Ginny longs for Logan, while he fights against Sebastian's maneuvering. And Hector, newly freed from prison, heads back to Storm...

Lightning Strikes by Lexi Blake
As Ian Briggs begins to fall for Marisol, Joanne and Dillon also grow closer. Joanne's new confidence spreads to Dakota but Hector's return upends everything. A public confrontation between Marcus and Hector endangers his relationship with Brittany, and Dakota reverts to form. Meanwhile, the Senator threatens Ginny and the baby...

Fire and Rain by R.K. Lilley
As Celeste Salt continues to unravel in the wake of Jacob's death, Travis grows closer with Kristin. Lacey realizes the error of her ways but is afraid it's too late for reconciliation with her friends. Marcus and Brittany struggle with the continued fallout of Hector's return, while Chase and Anna Mae face some hard truths about their past...

Quiet Storm by Julie Kenner
As Mallory Alvarez and Luis Moreno grow closer, Lacey longs for forgiveness. Brittany and Marcus have a true meeting

of hearts. Meanwhile, Jeffry grapples with his father's failures and finds solace in unexpected arms. When things take a dangerous turn, Jeffry's mother and sister, as well as his friends, unite behind him as the Senator threatens his son...

Blinding Rain by Elisabeth Naughton

As Tate Johnson struggles to deal with his brother's relationship with Hannah, hope asserts itself in an unexpected way. With the return of Delia Burke, Logan's old flame, Brittany and Marcus see an opportunity to help their friend. But when the evening takes an unexpected turn, Brittany finds herself doing the last thing she expected—coming face to face with Ginny...

Blue Skies by Dee Davis

As Celeste Salt struggles to pull herself and her family together, Dillon is called to the scene of a domestic dispute where Dakota is forced to face the truth about her father. While the Johnson's celebrate a big announcement, Ginny is rushed to the hospital where her baby's father is finally revealed...

Rising Storm, Midseason

After the Storm by Lexi Blake

In the wake of Dakota's revelations, the whole town is reeling. Ginny Moreno has lost everything. Logan Murphy is devastated by her lies. Brittany Rush sees her family in a horrifying new light. And nothing will ever be the same...

Distant Thunder by Larissa Ione

As Sebastian and Marylee plot to cover up Sebastian's sexual escapade, Ginny and Dakota continue to reel from the fallout of Dakota's announcement. But it is the Rush family that's left to pick up the pieces as Payton, Brittany and Jeffry each cope with Sebastian's betrayal in their own way...

Rising Storm, Season One

Tempest Rising by Julie Kenner
Ginny Moreno didn't mean to do it, but when she came home to Storm, she brought the tempest with her. And now everyone will be caught in its fury…

White Lightning by Lexi Blake
As the citizens of Storm, Texas, sway in the wake of the death of one of their own, Daddy's girl Dakota Alvarez also reels from an unexpected family crisis... and finds consolation in a most unexpected place.

Crosswinds by Elisabeth Naughton
Lacey Salt's world shattered with the death of her brother, and now the usually sweet-tempered girl is determined to take back some control—even if that means sabotaging her best friend, Mallory, and Mallory's new boyfriend, Luis.

Dance in the Wind by Jennifer Probst
During his time in Afghanistan, Logan Murphy has endured the unthinkable, but reentering civilian life in Storm is harder than he imagined. But when he is reacquainted with Ginny Moreno, a woman who has survived terrors of her own, he feels the first stirrings of hope.

Calm Before the Storm by Larissa Ione
Marcus Alvarez fled Storm when his father's drinking drove him over the edge. With his mother and sisters in crisis, Marcus is forced to return to the town he thought he'd left behind. But it is his attraction to a very grown up Brittany Rush that just might be enough to guarantee that he stays.

Take the Storm by Rebecca Zanetti
Marisol Moreno has spent her youth taking care of her younger siblings. Now, with her sister, Ginny, in crisis, and her brother in the throes of his first real relationship, she doesn't

have time for anything else. Especially not the overtures of the incredibly compelling Patrick Murphy.

Weather the Storm by Lisa Mondello

Bryce Douglas faces a crisis of faith when his idyllic view of his family is challenged with his son's diagnosis of autism. Instead of accepting his wife and her tight-knit family's comfort, he pushes them away, fears from his past threatening to undo the happiness he's found in his present.

Thunder Rolls by Dee Davis

In the season finale ...

As Hannah Grossman grapples with the very real possibility that she is dating one Johnson brother while secretly in love with another, the entire town prepares for Founders Day. The building tempest threatens not just Hannah's relationship with Tucker and Tate, but everyone in Storm as dire revelations threaten to tear the town apart.

1001 Dark Nights

Welcome to 1001 Dark Nights… a collection of novellas that are breathtakingly sexy and magically romantic. Some are paranormal, some are erotic. Each and every one is compelling and page turning.

Inspired by the exotic tales of The Arabian Nights, 1001 Dark Nights features *New York Times* and *USA Today* bestselling authors.

In the original, Scheherazade desperately attempts to entertain her husband, the King of Persia, with nightly stories so that he will postpone her execution.

In our version, month after month, each of our fabulous authors puts a unique spin on the premise and creates a tale that a new Scheherazade tells long into the dark, dark night.

For more information about 1001 Dark Nights, visit www.1001DarkNights.com.

On behalf of Rising Storm,

Liz Berry, M.J. Rose, Julie Kenner & Dee Davis would like to thank ~

Steve Berry
Doug Scofield
Melissa Rheinlander
Kim Guidroz
Jillian Stein
InkSlinger PR
Asha Hossain
Chris Graham
Pamela Jamison
Fedora Chen
Jessica Johns
Dylan Stockton
Richard Blake
The Dinner Party Show
and Simon Lipskar

44442683R00073

Made in the USA
Middletown, DE
07 June 2017